ETERNAL KINGDOM
A VAMPIRE NOVEL

Michele Roger

Michele Roger

ACKNOWLEDGEMENTS

My thanks go out to the many Kiwis, who have shared their culture, dedicated work ethic, and genuine love of life with me.

ALSO BY THE AUTHOR
THE CONSERVATORY

Chapter 1

Quinn sat down in the chair in the middle of the room. While vampires had not had a ruler or leader for over a millennium, a summons from the Council was serious. Sitting in the only chair in the room made it feel like a terrorist interrogation. In front of him sat the three chief members of the Council, each with faces filled with disapproval.

Guards—newly converted vampires with enormous strength and little patience—lined the walls. A dim light hung over him and another over the Council.

"We've invited you here today, Mr. Quinn, regarding the matter of a charge of yours. A Mr. James Bangor."

Quinn shifted slightly in his chair. Within himself, he contained an emulsion of fear, anger and elation. A side door opened and James, wrapped in helio-bonds, was dragged in by two guards. Quinn's heart leapt.

In the instant he saw James, Quinn wanted nothing more than to wrap his arms around the man, and simultaneously rip his throat open in rage. As the Council addressed James, Quinn stared at his lover and reminded himself that love was the most loathing and pathetic of illnesses.

The Council re-directed their questioning. "Now, Mr. Quinn, when was the last time you saw Mr. Bangor?" a member named Ruth asked. She was stunningly beautiful, wearing all black, her hair as red as blood.

"Over a year ago," Quinn admitted.

"Had you released him from your charge?"

"No," Quinn answered sheepishly.

"Your convert left your charge prematurely for over a year, yet you didn't report it; is that correct?"

Quinn stared down into his hands and confessed. His southern drawl was slow and his words elongated. "I didn't report it to the Council because I assumed Jam—err, Mr. Bangor, would come to his senses and return to his studies under my care. I know full well the punishment for not reporting a young rogue's escape. But I felt certain that he would return to his senses and come home."

"You knew the law and yet you broke it," another Council member, Jeremiah, spat. "Let me bring to light for you and Mr. Bangor what your failure to follow protocol has done."

A large screen came to life to the left of the Council. A blue-gray video, clearly from a security camera, began to play. It was James, fit, well dressed, just like Quinn remembered him. James was stalking his prey in the footage; a thin, sallow man. James' lean, muscular body rippled under his tight, gray t-shirt as he approached the pale man. Before the security camera, James appeared to be having an innocent conversation with the lesser-dressed man. The two men in the video exchanged a few laughs and after a few minutes, James handed the man a small item. At this, Quinn exhaled in disappointment. He knew what was about to play out.

It took only seconds for the thin, pale man to wrap an elastic around Quinn's forearm and jab the needle James had given him into his arm, directly over a vein.

The James on the video shifted back and forth with anticipation. He watched the man as he slumped down the wall into a seated position, and said a few words. James paced in the confines of the alley as he watched the heroin run through the man's blood stream. As the overdose began to take effect, the man fell over, and James pounced.

In a bizarre reenactment of the scene, James gave into his own uncontrollable addiction. There was an agitation as he waited for the drugs to enter the man's body, the build-up of anticipation as

James imagined the heroin-filled blood pumping through the heart, the saturation of the body as the blood reached the brain of his victim. Then, James went in.

The victim's jugular was swollen from the overdose. James bit into the artery and drank deeply. He twisted and contorted the addict's body to squeeze every last ounce of the heroin-laced nectar from him. Then, high and without care, the James in the video left the body out in the open, with its definitive marks of a vampire left in plain sight to later be discovered by a bouncer from the night club.

The screen went blank and Ruth looked at the present-day James with a rage brewing just under the surface. "Mr. Bangor, did you have a heroin addiction when you met Mr. Quinn?"

James said nothing.

Jeremiah presented the question again, but James gave no response. Quinn cleared his throat in encouragement. Ruth held up her hand in a gesture demanding silence from Quinn. Jeremiah stood and pointed a small penlight device at James and the helio-bonds around his neck instantly came to life. Radiant sunlight trapped in his cuffs cooked away the first few layers of his flesh, making a searing sound as they did so. Quinn gasped in empathy and horror as James fell to his knees in pain.

"You've been asked a question," Jeremiah said with rage at the precipice in his voice, "Answer!"

"Yes," James said, his voice weak.

Jeremiah turned slightly in his chair to look at Quinn. "Did you give the fool any instruction as to avoiding detection in the age of security cameras and digital media? Did you ever strive to make the point that our way of life must be kept secret to maintain our survival as a species?"

"There was some instruction, yes," Quinn stammered. "All modern day hunting demands the utmost scrutiny of the situation."

"You knew of this drug addiction and you hid it from the Council?" Jeremiah asked. "You let a rogue vampire run loose who clearly had little regard for our laws or way of life? One who clearly was unable to quench his newly-attained thirst, compounded with an insatiable appetite for a human drug? Is this correct?"

Quinn ran his fingers through his thick, black hair and straightened his tie. "Yes, sir."

"As is custom to our laws, you know that the fault lies solely with you, Mr. Quinn. If you had the audacity to convert a human to this eternity, then you're responsible for that charge until they are fit to abide by the rules set in place long ago. It's the only way."

"I take full responsibility for the severe indiscretion," Quinn replied humbly. He stared at James, who looked weak from the solar-powered bonds and completely unaware of the gravity of the moment. "May I address the room before my sentencing?"

Jeremiah nodded and Quinn stood. He smoothed out his suit and squared his shoulders.

James noticed Quinn had donned the one remaining treasure from his days as a soldier in the Civil War: his Medal of Honor.

Quinn straightened the medal and began. "It would seem that life takes on a certain focus for each individual who walks this earth. Some spend their time saturated in the helping of the less fortunate. Some surround themselves in art and music. I have admired those who could find fulfillment in those pursuits. I dare say, I even envied them. I am inclined to a different, darker road. Alive, I lived by the code of a soldier: kill or be killed. I plotted, hunted and destroyed my targets by day and scrubbed the blood from my stained hands by night. Not much has changed for me as a member of the undead, save my reasons for applying my skills became far less complicated. Survival. Pure and simple." Quinn turned to James. "I'm no poet. My school house teacher chased me with a switch because I refused to write a single essay." Quinn stopped to smile. He stared at James sincerely as tears welled up in the old soldier's eyes. "But when I met James Bangor, for the first time in all my eternity, I saw something beautiful. Killing lost its allure and blood was merely a way to feed. The world had far more to offer than the hunt of prey. James taught me that I could devote a hundred lifetimes to taking care of someone less fortunate than myself." Quinn paused and drew in a jagged breath and turned to the Council. "Without sounding contrite, my only defense for not informing the Council of Mr. Bangor's disappearance is that I knew the consequences of his actions. I knew he would be hunted, and I loved him too much to see that happen. It falls on deaf ears, but I had sincerely hoped that James would come to his senses and come home." Quinn turned once more, this time staring at the floor and caressing the edges of his medal. "I'm sorry. I never loved anyone before. I didn't know how and I failed. But I did try with the utmost sincerity."

The room was silent for several long minutes. Jeremiah closed his eyes as if in prayer. Ruth drummed her perfectly-manicured fingernails on the table in contemplation. Then, the Council members stood in unison.

"Mr. Quinn, please prepare for your sentencing," Ruth said.

Quinn stared at the Council as he stood at attention and replied, "I'm ready. What are my orders?"

"The Council then sentences you, Mr. Quinn, to immediate termination....Death by Light."

James looked up in alarm, whipping his head round to stare wild-eyed at Quinn. He began to fight the guards and protest, "No! Please! It's my fault...it's my fault!"

Ruth pointed the small pen device at James and his helio-bonds glowed brightly. Smoke rose from wherever the restraints touched James' skin. His knees buckled from the searing of his feet. His hands trembled as the cuffs cooked away at his wrists and arms. When James was silenced and fully prostrated on the floor, gasping, Ruth reduced the strength of the solar-based restraints.

Guards clad in leather gloves, jackets, pants and Kevlar masks forced Quinn into his chair. James began to sob loudly from the floor. Quinn and his chair were carried to the outermost corner of the far wall. James watched as the Council and the remainder of the guards donned thick goggles, leather sheaths and gloves.

James was unaware of the protective cloth the guards haphazardly wrapped around him. He stared terrified at the quiet, calm man who faced the wall. In the last second, Quinn turned to look at James. A small smile crossed the elder man's face as if to reassure his charge one last time.

The solid steel wall slid open to the outside, revealing a pre-eminent dawn. The heavily gloved guards tore away at Quinn's tie and ripped away his tailored suit jacket and silk shirt. His belt was removed, and a guard used it to secure him to the chair. Next, the guards removed all of the clothes from his lower torso. Quinn faced the rising sun without a fight. James and the Council watched as Quinn stared the morning sun down with every ounce of dignity a soldier could exude. He bravely fought the urge to scream as the morning sunlight hit his face. His body shook as he tried to maintain his composure. Fully exposed and vulnerable, Quinn gave in to agony. As the morning sun rose higher in the sky, its radiant light bore holes in his chest. He choked and writhed, raising his arms up in a feeble attempt to shield himself.

James could see light shining through Quinn's body. Blackened flesh hung off of his bones. Smoke enveloped Quinn, his screams of agony filling the room. As the heat and radiation peaked, Quinn burst into flames. The clothes at his feet acted as kindling.

James fought the urge to vomit as the smell of burning flesh hit his nostrils. Soon, Quinn's screams died and silence filled the stark room. James looked on at the fire that was the wooden chair and Quinn's corpse. Flame slowly turned to smoldering embers. Guards nodded to the Council to confirm he was dead, despite all that remained of Quinn being a pile of ash. The door was shut tight, leaving the wind to carry away the vampire's remains.

Broken and sobbing, the guards dragged James closer to the Council members. Jeremiah stared at the man with disdain. "You see, what Quinn tried to teach you by gentle example, vampiric law will teach you by swift and just punishment. You will remain in incarceration until such time you are found useful." The man waved to the guards and James was carried away to be returned to his cell.

With the guards dismissed, the Council convened in secret session. "I'm not sure I can stomach another hundred or so of those," Jeremiah remarked gloomily. "Quinn was a friend."

Ruth sighed. "Another twenty of those and word will spread like wild fire. There will surely be revolution."

"I've held my tongue throughout these proceedings thus far as I'm new to this post," the third member, Micah, declared in a high-pitched voice. "The facts and figures remain. We've never been the kind to hold or imprison. The cost is killing what little budget has been set aside for disciplinary measures. I've contacted the Councils of Spain and Turkey, Japan and Romania. They all have similar issues of young vampires not only caught on surveillance cameras, but also on cell phone videos. We must improve our ability to conceal our identities with the changing present day demands. Unfortunately, it would seem the latest figures point to a defect in our evolutionary ability to adapt fast enough. Too many are being noticed, caught on camera, driven by hunger or driven mad with starvation for fear of being caught. We face an incarceration and rehabilitation problem the likes of which we haven't seen in our history. We need a way to feed the ones we've found who have been driven to madness, and we need to rid ourselves of those who will not adapt to far more discretionary methods."

"In the past, we've merely made examples of those who have stepped out of the fringe," Ruth added hopefully. "Let the others in the *facility* listen to James' sobs for a while."

Jeremiah stood up. "This isn't a matter of one or two problems. There are at least two dozen cases before this Council. If Micah's research is correct, it appears to be a global epidemic. Much of them are like James and his blatant disregard for keeping our existence a secret. We're not designed to make our own kind live on the blood of rats. We're not the kind to imprison. It's a disgrace to us. Let the humans judge their own kind. I would rather live by the sword. While we can't let the world discover who and what we really are, surely a solution is before us. Execution at the rate of necessity will inspire revolution. A vampiric war would surely catch the interest of the human-digital world."

Ruth called for the guards, who stood just outside the door. She gave Micah a slight sneer. "I have never believed in statistics or numbers. Let me see the crisis first hand." She ordered one of the guards, "Tell your captain that the Council is adjourning to the *facility*, where we request a tour. You will take us now. This is far too serious to leave to numerical figures and a wealthy accountant."

Micah's long strides quickly took him through the thick double doors into the *facility*. He was immediately overwhelmed by the stench. The air, heavy from lack of ventilation, reeked of death and decay. Cries for mercy echoed down the makeshift prison corridor. Solar bonds formed an impenetrable seal at each bar, door and lock of every cell. Daily exposure weakened the vampire prisoners inside, who also wore the solar bonds around their neck and wrists.

The captain took the lead, his muddy jacket, tattered and trailing behind him. Ruth reminded herself to make note. Whatever they were paying him, they should double it. "Members of the Council, welcome to Hell," the captain said, his mouth forming a sadistic smile. He gestured for them to follow. Ruth wrapped her leather coat tight against her sleek body. She could feel the effect of the sun's channeled energy in the sealed doors of the cells as she passed by them. Jeremiah withdrew a pair of sunglasses from his pocket and wore them in the otherwise dark grouping of cells.

As they passed, they peered into the cells as the captain rattled off each of the prisoner's crimes. "This one was caught on a city traffic camera, drinking the blood of a woman he had just screwed in the back seat of a car. This one was posing as a doctor at the free clinic; administrative cameras caught her stealing sleeping pills. Our clever friend here would drop them in the drinks of healthy young men at the bar after hours. Her victims would pass out at the wheel, crashing their cars. She would arrive on the scene and clear the crowd, announcing she was a doctor. Then the good doctor would murder the man before the ambulance could arrive."

Micah seemed impressed as they made their way to the next cell block.

Some of the vampires looked up with haggard, desperate faces. Some lay on the mud floor, never bothering to acknowledge the visitors at all. A few rushed the bars, calling out for help, only to be burned by the solar energy.

One prisoner wildly gripped the bars filled with channeled sunlight. His hands immediately began to smoke, his flesh turning black and charred. "Blood!" he screamed! His face was twisted and contorted, disfigured from starvation and madness. He pressed his face against the cell door, burning it while he snapped his jaws and jagged teeth in a virtual bite. The Council members looked on in horror as the prisoner ignored his incinerating body for the chance to beg for a feed. Jeremiah and Micah stepped back from the man and walked on ahead with disgust. Something stirred inside of Ruth. She knew full well he would never heal his mangled hands without blood to drink. Pulling her leather sleeve up from her wrist, she called for the guard to open the prisoner's cell.

The prisoner began to weep and he fell to the floor, released from the torture of the persistent solar energy. "Give me your knife," she ordered the guard. The new vampire didn't move. Instead, he laughed. "How dare you disobey an Elder!" she screamed. Before the guard realized the situation, Ruth had relieved him of two spare helio-bond cuffs. Opening the half, moon-shaped rings, she plunged one half circle up into the guard's nose and sinus cavity. The thrust of her action sent the guard falling to the floor. The other bond she snapped into a ring and shoved down the guard's pants, where it hung from his member. Gasping and coughing, the guard tried to speak but soon his garbled talk turned to screams as Ruth found the remote and made the bonds active with a press of the button. She relieved the thrashing guard of his silver knife.

Standing over the prisoner, she made a small cut in her wrist and let a few drops of her blood fall into the prisoner's mouth. As he reached up to grasp her arm, she pulled away. "What I've given you will heal your wounds."

A flick of the remote again and the prisoner was under the strict confines of his helio-bonds. Ruth then turned to the smoldering prison guard and released him. "Take him and help him get a proper feeding," she announced. Several guards arrived to carry him away.

The captain said nothing for fear of any further wrath. Instead, he led the members deeper into the *facility*. The screams grew with ferocity and echoed off the mildewed walls. Some clawed at their mud floors in search of the blood of live worms and insects. Most of them ate mud in their deprived delirium. Unable to die but not really living without blood to drink, it was a purgatory the likes that Dante had not fathomed.

"Enough," Ruth said, holding up her hand to the guard leading the tour. She turned to the others. "How many inmates are we housing, Captain?"

"At this *facility*?" the captain asked.

Jeremiah gasped. "There's more than just this one?"

The captain gulped and shot a nervous glance to Micah. "I approved funding for the captain to procure whatever empty buildings he could allocate and fit with helio-based technology. So far we have roughly sixty in total throughout the United States."

Micah tried to cushion the staggering statistics. "The Canadian Council houses the truly starved and insane in their Alberta *facility* for us, in an act of good will. Nearly every country has had to implement similar lockups for those caught and unwilling to hide their hunts and kills."

Back in their meeting room, Ruth read Micah's facts and testimonies of other Councils throughout the world. They were all faced with similar challenges due to the digital age. Jeremiah paced while Micah sat bewildered at all the fuss.

Jeremiah drew a deep breath and sighed. "The last time our kind saw this much unrest and defiant behavior was in the Roman Empire. The liberties of that society seeped into vampiric culture. While the Romans were feasting and vomiting, vampires were drinking the blood of their victims in the middle of the street....often for show. Humans soon discovered who and what we were and hunted us with a ferocity and cruelty not measured by any modern day standard."

"How did you solve the problem back then?" Micah asked sheepishly.

Jeremiah pulled a large book from his satchel and let it land on the table with a thud. He flipped through the yellowing, onion skin pages until he found a picture and showed it to Micah and Ruth. "We took the worst offenders to the Coliseum. Archers lined the entire arena. Rome offered her most famous criminals and in the most fantastic display of public trials, the two sides played a life size game of chess. The game was played out between Julius Caesar and a skilled vampire by the name of Cadel. For every 'piece' taken, the archers shot human or vampire alike with a hundred flaming arrows." As Jeremiah recalled the game, Ruth watched him revel in its glories and triumphs.

"Who won?" Micah asked, at the edge of his seat.

Ruth noticed the two hunched over the book. "Oh, how the crowds cheered!" Jeremiah laughed. "Of course, the vampires won and took a vow that their few remaining numbers would leave the empire and fall into obscurity. And vanish they did. There isn't any mention of vampires in any great detail until Vlad the Impaler. Of course, I digress. A game like that could never take place in these times. We're trying to hide, not create a spectacle."

Micah returned to his numerical figures. He handed the other two graphs showing each purchase of an abandoned building and its residual value in the real estate market. Jeremiah read the itemized lists.

Ruth was still playing out the idea of a life size game. "Is it really so out of the question? How do you hide from a hunter?" she interrupted.

"What are you talking about?" Jeremiah asked. Ruth repeated the question and he answered easily. "You stand out in the open."

Ruth's epiphany came to light and Jeremiah opened his mouth to protest but couldn't find his way to an argument.

Ruth smiled. "It would have to be played in the most secure of places. It would require global cooperation from every contact and Council we have. But it must be done nevertheless, for the good of both human and vampire, for the setting of a new precedent in the modern age. There will be consequences in our secret world if one cannot behave in the open. We are clearly in our most desperate hour, Jeremiah. It's time to resurrect that glorious, ancient tradition. The Council must declare... *A game.*"

Chapter 2

The stadium shook from its concrete foundations up to the announcer's box and through the battered chair at Jim McCormick's window seat. The wooden, antique seat had sailed across the room too many times to count in the excitement of countless nail-biter endings in past tight rugby matches. This game was far worse. Two of the best, rival teams had scores climbing point for point on either side. The World Cup championship was on the line and the beat-up old chair flew across the announcer's box and landed, feet up, in the corner as Jim kneeled on the counter. His face and microphone headset pressed against the glass as he described the play on the pitch.

"The pass goes to Tree Trunks as the clock winds down to naught! The ball is still in play, folks. There's just a few meters of hope left for the Wallabies. Good luck catching this *All Blacks* farm boy from the Wiarapa. Just look at those legs!" Jim hollered, becoming hoarse. In under a minute, Stadium New Zealand thundered with cheers. Jim joined the throng of ecstatic fans announcing, "Tree Trunks Davies delivers the win as he crosses and makes the winning try at the World Cup for the New Zealand *All Blacks!*"

Helen Davies had been watching from the team suite and found herself in a rare display of affectionate happiness as she hugged her husband's manager, Ray Hanslow.

"There's no stopping our boy now!" Ray laughed.

Helen smiled as she peeled his groping hands off of her gratuitous bottom.

"We're set for life," he said. "The endorsements alone will bring in seven figures!"

"Seven figures? Who's tapped Robby?" Helen asked wearily, nearly wincing. It was always the same old locals trying to make good on Robby's humble beginnings. "It isn't another tractor commercial, is it? Tractors don't deliver seven figures, Ray." She said it loud enough to make a few of the happy supporters find their way to the other side of the room.

Ray's hands returned to Helen's lower back as he leaned in to whisper in her ear. "You haven't got many friends, Helen. Don't make an enemy out of me. To the press and the world you're the good, Christian farm wife of Tree Trunks Davies, but I know who you really are." Helen turned her head and looked straight at Ray as if to challenge him to continue. "Your French manicured nails and your Louis Vuitton sunglasses are just the tip of the iceberg. Your cash cow just won the fucking World Cup and I'm the man who has his ear...and his loyalty." Ray gripped her wrist tightly and pulled her ear close to his mouth. "Now, if you're a good girl, I may be able to talk that Mercedes dealership into two cars, eh? You'd look good in a convertible." She pulled away slightly but didn't remove Ray's wandering hand. "You give me what I want and I'll return the bloody favor. I have a long list of demands and my first is tonight. Robby needs some wife TLC. Why don't you go slip into something a bit sexier and make sure the golden boy is made happy tonight. Be a good wife and I'll make sure you get everything you deserve."

The room was full of beer-swilling suits from the ball club; big contributors waiting to congratulate the team and their captain. Helen quietly made her way up to the private suite without anyone taking notice, and waited upstairs for her husband. In the suite, she poured a glass of wine and filled the tub with hot, soapy water. With a long night ahead of her, she indulged in the spa amenities.

To her surprise, Robby came bursting through the door, interrupting her bath. He laughed happily upon finding her naked. "This day just keeps getting better!" He started peeling off his shirt and compression shorts. He stopped short to kiss her hard. His kiss tasted of beer and sweat.

"Don't you have interviews?" she asked as soon as he returned to stripping off his clothes. While she was willing to meet Ray's laundry list to keep Robby happy, she had hoped for a hot bath and a few Chardonnays before she had to bed him.

"Your husband just scores the winning try for the World Cup and comes in to kiss you and you're worried about the bloody interviews?" He looked crestfallen and for a moment, Helen felt bad. Robby pulled off his socks and a cake of dried mud fell onto the slate, bathroom tile.

"You're not coming in here are you?" Helen asked, putting her hands protectively over her bubbles as if they were her fortress.

"Why not?" Robby asked enticingly, sauntering over to the tub with a tipsy swagger in his step.

Helen stared at his filthy body covered in dirt, mud, sweat and blood with revolt. "Whatever you wash off in here, I'll be soaking in once you're out," she protested.

Robby stopped his feeble attempt to seduce his wife. He mumbled something under his breath and stomped over to the shower, turning the nozzle on full blast while he shook his head in brewing anger. He whipped around to stare Helen directly in the eyes. The success of the day and a few beers had loosened his tongue and lessened his patience. "I'm standing on the edge of middle age and yet I'm in the best shape of my life. Do you know how many women wish their husbands had half the physique I have? A few minutes ago, I just won the fucking World Cup! The money is pouring in. Long gone are the days of helping to milk the cows on the dairy farm, Helen. You want for nothing, thanks to me! All I wanted was to celebrate with my fuckin' wife! You're right. I don't want to come into the tub with you. The water is probably as cold as ice. Just like you!" He was shouting by the end of his speech where upon he slammed the glass shower door.

Helen sat in the suds, her heart pounding. They had spent so little time together since Robby had gone on the road that it was shocking to hear him yell. She pulled herself out of the suds and wrapped a towel around her body. She stopped and stared at her reflection in the mirror and barely recognized herself. Her fingernails were perfect like Ray said, nothing like her hands when she and Robby had run the dairy. Her hair had professional highlights; her figure was fuller from all of the celebrating and social event food and drink. If she didn't fuck him tonight, certainly some other woman would, gladly. If the other women only knew how lonely her life had been. If they knew how difficult it was to be married to an all star.

"They wouldn't think twice about bedding him. The hours of boredom sitting in hotel rooms all over the world." Robby had suggested she head a charity like some of the other wives, but what was she supposed to do, adopt an orphan?

Thinking of his celebrity status reminded her of what Ray had said downstairs. They were playing in the big leagues now. Helen stared back at herself in the mirror. Was she ready to go back to being a farmer's wife? Or was she willing to play her role in a game much larger than the rugby field? Finding her wine next to the tub, she drank the glass in one large gulp. She took a deep breath and returned to the mirror. She unwrapped the towel from her body and pulled at the clip in her hair. Her golden locks fell to her shoulders, just the way Robby liked it.

Opening the shower door, steam billowed out into the bathroom. She pulled it shut and stood behind her husband. In the confines of the shower, she could see the bruises forming on his

17

shoulders. She kissed them gently and she wrapped her arms around his chest. He didn't respond. Clearly, she had her work cut out for her, if she was going to quell his anger.

She slowly ran her perfectly-manicured fingertips down his six pack abs and kissed his spine. A low moan escaped his lips and Helen knew she had control once more. It was too easy, really. In a relationship, there was always one who loved more, one who was more deeply devoted than the other. Robby was as loving and loyal as a Labrador. Sure, he annoyed her with his canine, wide-eyed neediness, but all the same, he had out-performed her expectations, and that deserved a reward. Moving her hands slowly down to his groin, she caressed him until he was firm in her hand. He tried to turn to face and kiss her, but she insisted on staying the course. Slowly at first and then quickening her touch, she watched as his muscular forearms rippled and his hands gripped the tile wall. She quickened her motion until she felt his entire body tense. He stretched his neck and tilted his head back towards her. With her free hand she guided his head so her lips met his ear, kissing the lobe and whispering to him. His hand clenched into a fist and he hit the wall. She let the warm water run over him and her hand as he finished, exhaling and leaning back into her breasts as he relaxed.

He turned to her, switching places so that the hot water might warm her skin. "Now that's a better start to the night," he said and he almost sounded happy. She knew by morning the whole fight and her open disdain for him would be forgotten. He kissed the top of her head and stepped out into the bathroom, toweling his hair as he went to the bedroom. "Hurry up. Ray will be chomping at the bit for us to mingle."

Helen half-smiled, wrapping herself from head to toe in towels in a moment of self consciousness. "You go 'head. I'll catch up to you. Just text me from the pub and I'll find you." She knew he wouldn't protest to an endless supply of flowing beer in his immediate future. She noticed his chest muscles bulking out of his silk, blue shirt. She congratulated herself on recommending he change to a tailored suit for his meeting with the press and public. Robby still wore it well, even bruised and battered after a game. Tree Trunks kissed his wife goodnight. He knew she would never venture far to find him for the rest of the evening.

The Brew on Quay Pub was packed to its rafters with fans of both *All Blacks* and *Wallabies*. The press, screaming girls, and fans too drunk to be allowed in by the bouncers, were held back by police and yellow tape. These were Robby's kind of people; the salt of the earth. He stood next to the roped-off area, signing autographs and taking selfies with girls brave enough to push the drunks out of their way. Ray stood to the side with an emulsion of envy and pride. It was hard to respect anyone who made millions by playing a game, but Robby was different. He still wore the watch his father gave him, when he could have traded it in for a Rolex. He took pictures, gave interviews, and visited farm kids in hospitals, whose families worked too much or lived too far to visit. Robby was true blue and Ray would follow that kind of man to the end of the earth.

Inside the pub, both All Black and Wallabies were laughing, analyzing the plays and all round getting mindlessly drunk with the locals and fans alike. Andy, one of the owners, sat back and counted his blessings in an unexpected tidal wave of prosperity. The winners were buying rounds for the losers and the two sides were competing to see who could drink more. It was an added bonus that his team had won and he had lightened the wallets of three particularly wealthy Aussies who had dared place hefty wagers on the game the night before.

When Tree Trunks Robby Davies walked in, the place exploded with cheers. There was no way in the world the *All Blacks* captain could possibly drink all the beers that had been bought for him, but God loved a man who would sincerely try. Robby was just the man for the job.

He shook the hands of friends and strangers. He hugged and kissed their wives. With Ray at his side, Robby recounted the thoughts going through his head in the last nine seconds of the game leading to the winning try. Making his way to each table, the story got bigger, the odds tougher, and the admiration for Tree Trunks grew deeper.

"I tried to fake out Nuke Lancaster. He runs defense so well you'd almost think he was an All Black....almost." Laughter erupted. "I told Ray here, maybe we should try to recruit him, but then I found out why they call him Nuke. The harder he farts the faster he runs! That guy smelled like rotten chickens in a sulfur factory when he tried to make a tackle." Even the Wallaby fans joined the table, all falling down with laughter.

Robby stumbled his way to the men's room to find a line of impatient patrons on the brink of a fist fight. So he blearily stumbled to the service entrance and opened the door to the back alley. Holding himself up with one hand and using the other hand to unzip his fly, his drunken brain had trouble focusing on little else.

When he was done, he was surprised to find three men standing behind him. "Hey, mate," he said to the closest one. "Are you a Spates or Tui man?" There was no reply from any of the three. "No worries then, I'll buy you a pitcher of each and let you decide when you're done." Robby began to make his way to the door, but one of the men leaned against it, keeping it closed.

"I'm afraid it would take a hell of a lot more than beer for you to pay me back, mate. You see, I lost a lot of bloody money on that game, no thanks to you." The taller man seethed with anger.

Robby swayed and giggled. "Uh-oh, in trouble with the wife, are you? No worries. Nothing a beer and a week on the couch can't fix." Even in his drunken stupor, Robby knew he was in a tight spot. Robby wondered where Ray could be and why his manager wasn't looking for him yet. "I bet my manager Ray can come up with something nice to smooth it over. Let's go talk to him."

"We already did," the man at the door said. "He thinks you might pass on the sports anchor job and play one more year."

A third man, who had been fuzzy in Robby's line of sight, suddenly stepped into the back door light. He was holding a shovel. "I think you need to remember your humble beginnings on the farm," the man said. "Tell me, Tree Trunks, what's this called?" As he asked the question, he swung the shovel in the air, the flat metal head making full contact with Robby's' lower spine. The world spun and Robby couldn't decipher between up or down as he fell to the ground. He felt the shovel again, and this time, the sharp corner penetrated his kidney. He tried to scream but his brain was too busy thinking of a way out, but the pain was so great and so instant that Robby instantly began to vomit. Two more hits and the world grew dark. He heard the squeak of the rusty hinges on the door. There was a lot of shouting, but Robby couldn't make out the words. Footsteps came towards him and then the pain enveloped him like thick, black tar. Then there was blackness and silence.

The first thing Robby Davies saw when he awoke was the exhausted and distraught face of Ray. He was saying something to him. Something about the press, about making a statement.

Davies felt detached. It was as if his mind were separate from his body. Was he dead? He wasn't sure. It certainly felt like he was floating. He searched the room for Helen. Why wasn't she there? A swarm of doctors and nurses hovered over him like bees conducting an orchestra with tubes and monitors.

As they reached their crescendo, Robby felt a wave of unconsciousness wash over him, and he was gone again.

Chapter 3

Ruth flipped impatiently between two channels. She hated to be kept waiting. Somewhere around her fifteenth analysis and sports highlight playback, the knock came at the door. Micah let himself in.

"You're late. Have you any idea how much I hate to wait?" Ruth hissed.

"Yes, but unlike you," Micah replied, "I haven't millions that I sit upon, cashing in on the mysterious deaths of my dead husbands every decade or so. I have to keep human hours in order to remain employed. I don't normally meet clients in the middle of the night."

Ruth turned the TV volume down and placed the remote on the designer ottoman. Micah was taken aback when she stood up. She was wearing a long, lace gown; a far cry from her leather coat and pants she wore for Council meetings. Micah wondered if it was custom made for her, as the see-through lace pattern seemed to reveal as well as conceal just the right amount of her porcelain skin.

"Is that what I am, a client?" she smirked. "And we both know this is exactly the kind of hours you keep. No one honest ever launders money or evades taxes by day," she mused.

"That's how I was elected to the Council, wasn't it? A vampire who happens to have found his way in the human world as an accountant, tied to the most prestigious banking firm in the country. I'm a man with no political ambitions and yet suddenly I get summoned and elected to the Council? I assume I've been tapped for my connections?" Micah surmised, dryly.

"I beg to differ. I think you underestimate your talents. I know potential when I see it, which is why I persuaded the other members."

"So the Council doesn't want something from me. You do," Micah said, trying to exude confidence. Truthfully, he had never been this close to such a beautiful woman. Becoming a vampire may have given him immortality, but it certainly hadn't made him handsome. He was lucky to screw an occasional ambitious intern at the office. Women of power or wealth rarely gave him a second glance.

"I would like to think that my helping hand up to a place of power makes us friends." She wiped her bottom lip with a red-polished fingertip. Micah noted that the shade matched her hair nearly perfectly. He was in way over his head. Sadly, he kind of liked the feeling.

"And friends help one another, right?" he asked, unable to hide his sarcasm.

Ruth smiled. "I do find cleverness extremely attractive." She took her finger from her lip and ran it down his tie. "Yes, I need a favor. It's not for me though. It's more for the game. I know that Jeremiah is working with the other world Councils on compiling a list of prisoners to play for the vampire side. But I'd like to use this act of...good will, to restore some of the confidence to the powers that be."

"Powers that be?" Micah asked, confused and nervous. Ruth rarely ever beat around the bush and he felt like she was testing him.

"You honestly don't believe that vampires have remained the topic of myth and entertainment for hundreds of years merely by chance, do you?" she asked. "There's a strong and confidential alliance between governments, private groups and anonymous individuals who help to keep vampires from being a mainstream reality in society's consciousness. Lately, that alliance has been skating on thin ice. I'd like to restore their confidence."

"You need money," Micah guessed.

Ruth laughed. "Your sex appeal is waning. You'll need to think on a grander scale if you want my affections, and my loyalty."

Micah tried to unscramble his thoughts. He thought about denying his attraction to her but it was ridiculous. He asked himself what was better than money. "You want power. How can I deliver it from where I'm standing?"

Ruth turned up the volume on the remote as the anchorman elaborated on the close-up of a handsome human man. "I need a hero. I need someone the human world can cheer for and believe in, against all odds." She handed Micah a cell phone. "Use this phone exclusively to contact only me. I've booked your flight to Auckland. His manager's name is Ray."

Micah stared at the TV screen, listening to the commentary. He turned to Ruth, staring at her incredulously. "How do I convince an all star athlete to commit suicide?" he asked, exasperated at the impossible prospect.

"You're a numbers man. It's a gamble but a calculated risk in our favor. If by some miracle, the human team can find a chess master better than Cadel and they win, I'll personally convert the survivors myself."

"What are you saying?" he shouted. "We can't offer that! Jeremiah will never approve! There must be some law!"

"What rule?" she objected. "Tell me! Why can't we offer the ultimate prize: immortal life to any human willing to risk death in a human-sized game of chess between two masters?" Ruth's eyes blazed with anticipation. There was excitement in the high stakes odds.

In her red-eyed fury, she twisted Micah's tie into a slip knot noose. It wasn't a death threat, but he certainly could see that she had recently fed. By the strength of her grip, the victim had been young. Her strength was far superior to his. He could see that she was struggling to control her rage as she bared her teeth. "What that old fool Jeremiah doesn't know won't hurt him. Once the deal is set in place, you and I will vote him out on the matter. Isn't that right?"

"Yes," Micah squeaked.

Ruth instantly released him when he gave the answer she wanted to hear. "Now go, or you'll miss your flight. Don't come back until you have Robby Davies under locked contract. The humans need a king and they shall have one for whom they can devote their loyalties."

"This isn't Ancient Rome, you know."

Ruth disregarded and dismissed him with a wave of her hand.

Micah left Ruth's penthouse with what little dignity he had left intact.

Ruth studied a model board and pieces of 'The Game.' She placed the King for the white side in the center. With Robby Davies' fate sealed, it was time to call upon a hero of a different sort; a leader of convicts, a commander that the undead could respect and follow.

James was unrecognizable when the guards threw him at Ruth's feet. The captain reported that in James' bereavement, he'd spent the days ceaselessly throwing himself at the solar-powered bars of his cell. Every square inch of his body was charred, including his face. His hands were deteriorating and his fingers were curled, becoming disfigured. His botched-up suicide proved his naivety about being a vampire and would take a proper feeding to correct before Ruth could speak with him properly.

Ruth handed the captain a card. "Take him to this address and see that he's put to bed in the guest room to the left of the entry-way."

Madame, this is a prisoner of the..." the captain protested but Ruth cut him off.

"I know damn well whose prisoner he is because I sentenced him! Do as you're told and take him through the service entrance. Keep him under guard. I'll meet you there."

The only way to get James to the address was to strap his charred, emaciated body onto a stretcher held down with helio-injected bands. The captain doubted that they really needed to take the precaution, making James immobile, but in his line of work, he had learned it was better to be safe than sorry. As he drove the van through the dusk-filled streets, he could hear the faint whispers of the prisoner in the back. James was calling for Quinn, and asking for forgiveness in his delirium. Most prisoners called for help, or blood, or revenge, but rarely did they call for loved ones and never did they ask for forgiveness. It wasn't vam-piric. For a moment, the seasoned captain didn't know if he should kill the bastard for his weakness or respect him for still having some kind of a heart, albeit one that was no longer beating.

Upon arriving at the address given to him by Ruth, the captain wheeled the gurney into the service entrance and up to the pent-house floor. It took him no effort at all to lift James' feather-light body onto the guest bed in Ruth's apartment. James thanked the captain, calling him Quinn. The captain was taken aback. He had heard all the rumors swarming about the trial and the sentencing. Death by Light was the harshest sentence. The captain had per-sonally mourned the death of Quinn. They had been friends for over a century, and he respected Quinn's slowly-worded drawl and simple-minded logic. He wouldn't have called Quinn deep by any stretch, but he would have called him loyal, and that was as good a friend as any. Reaching into his pocket, he pulled out a small secret he had been carrying. Carefully prying open the scorched hand of James, he gingerly placed the only remnant of Quinn not carried away by the wind: the treasured Medal of Honor.

"Whatever that bitch has planned for you, James, I have no doubt it'll be a special kind of hell only Ruth can personally give. Keep this safe. I think Quinn would want you to have it," the captain whispered.

James seemed to understand and he gripped it tightly, otherwise lying in misery. The captain left James to his thoughts, stepping outside the room to keep guard as ordered and return to his duty.

It was likely that James would not take a feeding willingly, and he certainly was in no shape to hunt. If his mental state was truly suicidal, then it would take an irresistible temptation for Ruth to intercede effectively.

Ruth hit the button of her silver E-class to unlock the doors and jumped in. Hitting the Bluetooth as she left the *facility*, she made a phone call. "Hi, Zoe, it's me. I'm hungry for junk food. Where's a good spot to eat?"

"You know how I feel about junk food," Zoe replied. "If you don't know what it's been eating and drinking for at least the last three days, you shouldn't eat it."

"You were a chef too long before you turned, Zoe," Ruth said with a sly grin. "Still can't shake the old habits?" she mused.

Zoe's laugh came through the Bluetooth. "Principles are the same whether it's grass fed beef or fried food fed human. Meet me downtown. I've been watching a newly-divorced businessman who's been consuming nothing but caviar and sixty-five dollar a bottle Merlot this week. We can share the meal."

"It's not for me actually. It's for a friend," Ruth said.

"So you're looking for take out?"

"In every sense of the word. More like cheap steak and heroin."

"Boring...do you hate this friend? Or is this a call for comfort food?" Zoe asked.

"Go with that."

"Your pairings are always the most challenging. It's been years since I was into street food. Let me scout around and I'll call you in twenty. Head to the south side docks, I'll meet you there."

Sure enough, in her eternal pursuit of the ultimate gastric adventure, albeit blood-based, Zoe met Ruth at the Dockside Bar on the south side of town. Dressed in her typical little black dress and stilettos, Zoe maintained the look of a sexy twenty-year-old, even though she had been turned about a century ago. Ruth beamed with happiness as Zoe tapped the empty seat in the booth next to her. Two prime candidates were already seated across her table.

Ruth slid into the seat next to Zoe. She set her cell on the table, noticing the carvings made directly into the table surface. All appearances suggested the marks had been made by knife point. She smiled at Zoe. "This place is perfect. I love you."

"I know. Now, this is Tommy and this is Mike," Zoe smiled enthusiastically as she introduced the two men in the booth with her. "I was telling them how my friend and I just came into a bit of money and were looking for a good time and a little pick-me-up."

Ruth could smell the rusty stench of heroin seeping from the pores of the man sitting directly in front of her. His eyelids were lined red and he was rail thin...an experienced user. "Let me buy you boys some dinner first, and then the adventure begins. Steaks all round?" Ruth's suggestion was met with eager enthusiasm.

Ironically, both sides of the table felt as though they had hit the jackpot.

Lying in the guest bed in Ruth's penthouse apartment, James was daydreaming of Quinn. The two of them were lying under a pecan tree on Quinn's southern family estate. As the wind blew gently through the tall sweet grass, James could smell the honeysuckle in bloom. He could still hear Quinn humming some Appalachian tune he always sang as he began to relax. James laid his head on Quinn's chest and breathed in deep. The sudden strong smell of metal and rust filled his nostrils.

James felt the bed move in the darkness of the room. He realized the smell was not of his dreams but rather his reality.

Two figures were brushing against the bed as James lay silently in the blackness. As he listened, he could hear the pair kissing. His mind raced. Clearly someone had landed on the bed with a thump. The aroma was getting closer. The familiar smell was overwhelming and despite himself, James began to salivate. His eyes rolled back in his head as he tried to resist. It had been so long since he had been this close...so close to the two things he desired most next to death. He tried to think of something else. He imagined the pecan tree and Quinn, but all that remained in the forefront of his mind was the ever-growing smell of heroin and blood.

"Don't fight it, my darling. He's alive for the tasting. Feast before his heart bursts from the overdose," Ruth cooed in his ear. James dug his blackened nails into the down feather duvet as he tried to resist. His face contorted nevertheless, and his lips curled to make way for his elongated teeth.

Muffled sounds of protest came from Mike, the Dockside junky, as Ruth held him down at the end of the bed. She had her hand over his mouth. Mike was clearly unaware of his situation but wasn't so high not to sense he was in some kind of trouble.

Overwhelmed with grief and starvation, James gave in to his hunger and addiction. He found himself in a crouched position ready to pounce. Hunched over Mike, with his burned face and protruding teeth, James was truly a monster. Mike began screaming at the top of his lungs but Ruth muffled it as best she could by stuffing her fist into his mouth and punching his throat.

James sprang onto Mike and tore open the man's shirt. He drank directly from Mike's still beating heart. To Ruth's surprise, very little blood found its way to the sheets or carpeted floor as James consumed ravenously. She heard the man's bones creak as James bent Mike's body backwards. Mike's pelvis broke at the lower spine when James twisted his body to drink any drug-laced blood that may have pooled in the extremities. When Mike's corpse hit the floor, it was as white as a sheet and the skin clung to the bone from lack of moisture. When James was finished, the wounds around his mouth and eyes began to heal. James stared at Mike's broken and drained body in the darkness. His chest heaved and he began to sob.

Ruth rubbed the top of James' head much like a master to a dog. "Denial, anger, bargaining, depression and acceptance. You've come full circle, and now it's time to honor Quinn….and I have the perfect way for you to do so, too."

When Micah arrived at the hospital in Auckland, the outside corridors were swarming with press and fans. Security guards manned every elevator leading up to the fourth floor, where it was rumored, Robby Davies had just returned from a six hour surgery. Micah took shelter in the small chapel just off the lobby. He was beginning to get thirsty after the long night flight filled with unsuspecting humans. As was his custom, he had learned that if he could step away from temptation for even a short time, he could gather his reserves and wait until night fell to feed.

Sitting on a bench in the darkest corner of the room, Micah pictured himself peacefully sleeping in his coffin filled with soil from his childhood backyard. He promised himself that he would return for a rest immediately following this little junket. As he sat in a meditation of sorts, he heard the stern voice of a woman giving explicit directions. He slumped down in the bench to go unnoticed as the woman and whomever she was directing approached.

"Now, you listen to me, Father. There's too much money riding on this to let scruples get in the way. Robby doesn't need last rights; he needs to renew his wedding vows. That way, if he doesn't pull through, it's very clear who is his wife and sole survivor is. It needs to be made clear to his manager, the ball club, and his dirt-poor farm family."

"As his wife, Helen, are you not more concerned with the state of his soul than of his money?" the priest asked.

Micah slunk from shadow to shadow in the chapel until he made his way to the corridor just around the corner. The priest and the woman jumped as he startled them.

"Sorry." Micah raised his hands in surrender. "I was looking for the coffee machine and couldn't help overhearing your conversation."

"You could hear us?" Helen asked suspiciously.

Micah pulled a card from his inside jacket pocket. "I'm a licensed barrister. If you need a wedding with no questions asked, I'm sure we could arrange something," Micah schmoozed.

Helen read the card and returned her scrutinizing gaze to Micah. "And what sort of payment were you looking for?"

"The whole world loves your husband, Mrs. Davies. You're a super couple. I wish only to help, if I can, in any way. As a lawyer and accountant, I have a few connections. Just thinking I might be able to help your husband and yourself would be my honor."

Helen smiled. She took off the lanyard hanging round her neck, which held a card reading PASS on it. "I would be very grateful for your help. Robby is with his manager, Ray, in room 405. He's just waking up from his surgery."

Micah watched as the priest stormed away in frustration. Micah smiled ever so slightly. As he watched the priest return to the sacristy to prepare for a service, Micah turned to Helen and said, "I'm just going to grab a bite to eat and then I will meet you upstairs. You really should be there when your husband wakes up."

In under an hour, Micah, well fed on the blood of the holy man, and the priest's body delivered to the hospital incinerator to dispose of it, he smoothed out his suit and straightened his tie before walking into room 405. Helen introduced him to Ray and the two men shook hands while sizing each other up.

Impeccable timing smiled down on Micah as the surgeon, looking weary and nervous, pulled off his cap and put it in his scrub's pocket. "I know that you requested a meeting before we have to deal with the press," the surgeon said as he stood at Robby's bed side. "How are you feeling?"

"I could use a beer," Robby joked.

"Your spinal cord was severely damaged in two places and your right kidney was punctured, the surgeon explained. "Presently, your body is relying solely on your left kidney, which is the only reason I haven't prescribed you a beer." Everyone gave a nervous laugh and Ray slapped Robby on the shoulder, jabbing him in good fun.

"We were able to reconnect many of the severed nerves that go from your spine to your lower legs," the surgeon said. "You should start to have some feeling restored, or so we hope, by as early as tomorrow. With a lot of physical therapy, I think there's a very good chance you'll walk again." At this, the surgeon smiled. No one else joined him.

Helen cried and walked to the window.

"So what you're really saying, Doctor," Robby sighed, "is that my rugby career and days of being an athlete are over." He punched the metal railings of the hospital bed. It wasn't a question. He was simplifying the verdict.

"What I'm saying," the surgeon countered, with a good amount of sternness in his voice, "is that ten years ago, you would've been sentenced to a wheelchair for the rest of your life. Thanks to modern medicine and stem cell research, with some work and a good attitude, you'll be able to resume nearly a completely normal lifestyle."

Robby began to shake his head the way he did when anger was growing inside of him. He started to yell, his face turning beet red. "Do you have any idea what normal is for me? Me! Robby Davies! I've been on a rugby field since I was five bloody years old! Walking isn't good enough!" He turned his anger from the surgeon to Ray. "You want me to report the news when I just became the news! I finally made it! I had it in my hands, Ray, and now you people expect me to give it up and be thankful that I will bloody walk?" More pounding of his fists ensued as Robby raged on.

The surgeon left in frustration and soon returned with a syringe. Within seconds of the needle penetrating his IV, once again,

Robby Davies was consumed by oblivion. This time, he didn't fight it. Instead, he gladly welcomed it.

Waiting until the room had grown still and Helen had gone home for the night, Micah watched as Ray paced and wrote lists. As Ray paced, he ran his fingers through his hair and mumbled options and angles to himself. "I need to have a plan for when Robby wakes up; a good plan," he confessed to Micah. "That man has never had a day in his life when he wasn't working towards something he wanted. It's how he operates. It's hardwired into his brain. If he won't settle for a news anchor job and he won't ever play ball again, I have to think of a way to convince him to… what? Coach? Mentor? And the press. We have to give them something." Ray was talking faster and faster as his thoughts raced. "Not Robby. Not now. No." Ray turned to Micah desperately for any advice the quiet stranger could give.

"What about Helen?" Micah threw Ray a bone.

"Yes! Helen. We'll make her carry the image that Robby is making a great recovery. I'll tattoo a damn smile on that bitch if I have to. Then we'll call in specialists. The best the world has to offer, sparing no expense. Excuse me, I need to step outside and call my secretary. She needs to start researching the best spinal cord injury doctors." He paused then; he was mostly thinking out loud.

Micah smiled as he walked over to Ray and put his hands on the manager's shoulder. "I have a better idea. What I'm about to tell you will be unbelievable at first, but if you let me explain, it just might be the miracle your boy is hoping for."

Chapter 4

'The world is a vampire,' Ruth's phone rang, the ring tone a glorious tribute song by *The Smashing Pumpkins*.

It was a text message from Micah. `Ruth, Still in negotiations with Davies but the outcome looks like it'll go our way. Give me a few more days. Flying home to rejuvenate and then will return to resume negotiations.`

Ruth clicked her tongue in disgust. Micah was showing his weak side when she had little time or patience for delays. Her plan needed precision and not flights of fancy home to lie in an earth-filled coffin. She hit reply via voice call. When Micah picked up, she spoke in a controlled, direct tone. "My money isn't paying for trips back and forth across the globe!"

"It's unlawful to deny a fellow vampire their basic need to return to their home soil," he answered, feeling brave from being so far away. "I wouldn't want to have to mention it to Jeremiah the next time I see him."

There was a loud click as Ruth ended the conversation. Micah placed the phone in his pocket and boarded the red eye flight bound for Detroit.

"My name is Rose and I'll be guiding you through your rehabilitation," a lean, athletic woman said cheerily.

Robby smiled at her, and when she looked down at her chart, he glared angrily at Ray, who was looking on from a clear, safe distance.

Rose caught his eye and he smiled at her again. "Right, now did the physio department tell you that we recommend you have a partner? That way, you'll have someone who knows each exercise and how it's performed in the event that you need to complete your routine when I'm not here."

"Why wouldn't you be here?" Robby asked.

Rose paused, slightly nervous. "No reason in particular," she said, taking a deep breath. "Just a good idea. So, is it this bloke over here?" she laughed, directing the question to Ray. "If so, I'm afraid you're a bit overdressed in that suit and tie."

"Naw! It's not him!" Robby was quick to answer for Ray. "He's hopeless at just about everything. Well, maybe not storytelling. He likes to think he can turn real life people into superheroes and immortal gods in the stories he makes up. Isn't that right, Ray?"

Ray shrugged and reserved his anger. "Some of us believe in miracles and some of us don't. Obviously, you're not a believer, Robby. It's sad."

"No, it isn't! It's not sad at all. It's reality, Ray. I never took you for a gullible man."

Rose interrupted, trying to quell the hostility. "Are we waiting on your wife to arrive this morning? I saw her interview last night on TV. Is she running late? She might be."

Robby cut Rose off very abruptly. "No, just me. I've worked out all my life. I doubt there's something new you can show me. Let's just get to work."

Rose sensed the tension between Ray and Robby. Typically, it was hospital protocol to bring in the rotating physical therapist, which would help in her absence, but Rose could see a quick escape from the room was more important. "That's the spirit! Okay then, we're off to the rehab room," she announced to Ray. "We should be back in three quarters of an hour." Rose wheeled Robby out and the two strolled silently down the hall and into the elevator. Robby jumped at the loud echo inside the small space as Rose coughed several times, releasing her hand from his chair and applying the foot brakes so she could step away. When the coughing fit had ended, she wiped away her watering eyes and apologized.

The double doors opened and Rose wheeled Robby into the rehab room. He felt the chair foot brakes applied once again and looked around to see what was stopping them. Rose was adjusting a weight machine just above his head.

"I don't need to work my arms and chest, sweetheart. You must be reading that chart upside down," he joked. "It's not my arms that need help it's my legs that are buggered."

Rose continued to methodically set the weights. To his surprise, her small hands had immense strength as she slowly peeled his hands off the wheelchair armrests.

She spoke firmly but softly. There was something completely feminine about her that made Robby let go of a bit of his temper. "I need your upper body to be as strong as it can be," she explained. "If we're going to preserve your name as Tree Trunks then I have to know that your upper half can support you while we work the lower half."

An old man sitting in a recliner by the window shouted, "You can work my lower half anytime you want, honey!" The room of patients broke into laughter. Rose blushed despite herself.

"You'll have to forgive Mr. McGuiness. His whole life he was a police officer, a man in uniform, and he thinks he can still charm all the ladies." She said it loud enough for the old man across the room to hear as she adjusted Robby's hands on the weight machine grips.

"You can't blame the old boy for saying what the rest of the room was thinking," Robby said as he began to work the machine and give Rose a wink. For the first time in weeks, for a few, brief seconds, The World Cup Champion felt like his old self.

Micah was relieved to find that Ruth let her rage befuddle her mind. She never asked him why he never moved his coffin to the Council's central location in the heart of Chicago. Truth be told, he had left Detroit in such a hurry, he hadn't thought to bring it. For several years, he had tried to put the whole matter out of his head, but recently, his body had begun to crave the earth from home. Lord knows he had tried to supplement with the best organic mixture and fabricated coffin his promotion at work could buy.

He told himself that Chicago and Detroit were both Midwestern states, but the effect wasn't the same. Of late, every part of him, down to some metaphysical, molecular level, craved Detroit. He felt as if he would certainly whither away to nothing if he didn't get home immediately. Detroit had little to offer him, but dirt it had in spades.

Micah called Jacob. He was surprised to find his housekeeper very much awake and eager to talk, considering it was three in the morning.

"Master, have you landed? Shall I come to get you with the car?" Jacob asked gleefully.

"Yes, I've arrived, but I'll take a cab home. Have you left everything in place as I instructed?"

There was a long pause on the other end of the phone. Jacob's voice croaked as he answered, "Yes, but I truly wish you would let me take care of the mess before you return. Your sister..."

"No!" Micah shouted. "Leave it. I need to be reminded and you doing as you're told will help me to never forget."

"Yes, sir," Jacob trailed off, sounding meek and frightened.

Micah hung up and hailed a cab. Once inside, the cab traveled down I-94. He could have easily arranged for Jacob to bring the Mercedes, but Micah wanted to take in Detroit and its surrounding area alone in the silence only a stranger driving a passenger could bring. As the severely beat-up Crown Victoria cab made its way through the city, Micah could let his memory wander. "Take a detour through the city," he directed, nostalgically.

The lights from the newly-built casinos illuminated the sky. Motor City was the first one to stand out with its sleek, linear lighting resembling an electric serpent slithering up the building. Prostitutes lined Woodward Avenue in their tattered stockings and purple-died wigs. A few, Micah thought, he remembered, but he wasn't sure. Prostitutes had a short shelf life and the likelihood of some remaining alive and unscathed from his human days was highly improbable.

When he passed Orchestral Hall, Micah's mind flooded with thoughts of Emily. A lump formed in his throat. He remembered how lovely her black sequined dress had glittered under the spotlights as she played her cello there. He recalled his immense pride, and of only wishing he might show her off to his new friends. But it was far too dangerous, he had known it, but in that moment, while she took her bow in front of a standing ovation, he had just hoped some how it would all work out.

He laughed out loud to himself, making the cab driver look at him through the rearview mirror. If Micah had only known how very, very complicated it would become, he never would have kept the sort of company he did. Maybe then, he would still have her. Maybe...

As the city lights turned to lamp posts lining suburban streets, the mansions of Grosse Pointe stood importantly, puffing out their chests and imitating their original owners: captains of Detroit steel, coal and manufacturing. Mercedes, BMWs and Lexus kept the cab company at the stop light. Grosse Pointe was the east edge where Detroit's elite went into hiding. This wasn't the newsworthy part of the city and the residents paid the press and law enforcement through the nose to keep their troubles out of the spotlight.

As the cab driver pulled into the driveway, he couldn't help but whistle. "Nice digs, man."

"You should see the inside," Micah said proudly as he paid the fare.

Jacob opened the front door, smiling nervously. He was little more than nineteen, with wild, blonde hair and a willowy thin frame. He diverted his eyes so as not to make eye contact with Micah, but peeked from under hooded eyelids to read the vampire's expression.

Micah sniffed the air. "Ah good. You used the recipe of chemicals I emailed to you. I can tell."

Jacob smiled at making his master happy.

"Where is she?"

Panic flooded Jacob as he took Micah's coat. He pointed to the large music room. Ornate, mahogany carved walls filled the foyer and music room of the immense house. Oil paintings from their family, dating back to the early sixteenth century hung in a classical grouping over the eight-foot fire place. Emily was wearing her favorite red velvet dress, and lying on the couch. Jacob had poured her a glass of wine. Her shoes lay on the rug Micah had purchased in Istanbul. Micah kissed his sister hello.

Michele Roger

Her stark white skin was ice cold. He looked into her cloudy, blue eyes. Jacob stood in the corner of the room, cowering as he watched his master's inspection.

Carefully, Micah untied the silk scarf from around Emily's neck. He stared at the two puncture marks he had left deep in her skin. He would have cried at that moment if he could have found any way to begin to forgive himself. He slumped down next to her corpse and began to apologize over and over again. As he reached out to hug her, he brushed Emily's hair. Several of her brown locks disintegrated at the scalp and fell in a clump into Micah's hand.

Jacob wanted to run away as Micah reacted in panic and disillusionment. It suddenly felt as if all of the air had been sucked from the room. Micah's eyes were blood red and his face contorted in his seething. He searched the room frantically, looking for Jacob. In his remorse and bereavement, he looked more like a monster than a man. "You said you used the chemicals!" he screamed.

Jacob began to weep. "I did, sir. I swear I did. Just like you instructed. Please, sir, it's been years! I've kept her safe and preserved all this time." His weeping turned to sobbing as he dropped to his knees. "I burned the old, blood-soaked rug like you said and scrubbed the blood from the floors. I put down the new rug you sent. Then I put her in her favorite dress and injected the chemicals, following your every instruction. Please, sir!"

"Where is her cello?" Micah barked through bared teeth.

"It's there, by the piano." Jacob pointed with trembling hands.

"Play it."

"Oh, sir, I can't. I just can't."

"You were her student; now play it. Show me what she taught you!"

Micah's eyes blazed crimson and Jacob ran to the grand piano, where Emily's cello stood waiting. As Jacob played, Micah held the hand of the first victim he had ever killed as a vampire. Ironically, it was the only murder he ever regretted committing. Brother and sister lay on the couch together, listening to Jacob's concerto.

"I took the liberty of turning on a bit of inspiration for you this morning," Rose said cheerfully as Robby was wheeled into the rehab room.

He looked up at the television and there was Helen sitting in an over-stuffed chair.

"I heard she was giving an interview this morning," she said. "I figured you wouldn't want to miss it."

Robby had been hurt and left lonesome by Helen's absence. She had done as Ray instructed, making a positive statement to the press about Robby's recovery, but soon after had left without so much as a goodbye note. She didn't answer her cell and she hadn't inquired about his prognosis, according to the nurse's station. Seeing her on television, Robby felt a relief in knowing she was doing her duty, keeping him in the spotlight with interviews.

"Turn up the volume, will you?" Robby lay on the floor mat with his head turned towards the screen.

"Okay, now try to resist me," she said and stretched out his leg, with his foot straight up into the air. She felt no push back. On TV, Helen smiled sweetly as the anchor introduced her. The interview started as Rose bent Robby's foot to stretch his arch.

"It's a terrible tragedy about your husband. Have his attackers been found?" the newswoman asked.

Helen looked stern. "Robby's manager said that he saw three men fleeing the scene when he found my husband. So far, they've only questioned one possible suspect. No one's been arrested."

"From the security we've seen at the hospital, it looks like all of his fans are showing their support for a full recovery," the newswoman said positively, smiling into the camera.

"Yes, the letters, flowers and cards have really been good for Robby." Helen paused, taking a tissue from the table that was between her and the newswoman.

Rose told Robby to lie back down as he tried to sit up, watching his wife begin to cry on national television.

"It's just..." Helen sniffed, "I have no idea how we're going to pay for it all. I had no idea how much specialists and hospital bills and intense therapy could cost. At this rate, we'll lose everything we have trying to save his legs." She broke down and the cameraman zoomed in for a close-up. Instead of comforting Helen, the newswoman saw her chance for higher ratings and probed Helen deeper. "Do you think you'll have to go back to working the family dairy farm? Surely, your husband won't be able to conduct that level of physical labor, even if he does regain the ability to walk."

Rose could suddenly feel resistance pushing back in Robby's legs. The more he watched, the harder he pushed without even realizing it. Rose didn't know if she should be concerned or encouraged.

"I took my vows very seriously when I married Robby. In sickness and in health, and if running the farm is what I have to do to keep bread on the table, then that's what I'll do."

"So inspiring," the newswoman remarked, forgetting her impartiality. "Your husband might be watching right now; do you have a message for him?" The newsroom held its breath, ready to jump at the chance to replay whatever rating-boosting words

Helen might spew and lead with it on the eleven o' clock highlight hour.

Helen smiled directly into the camera with tears in her eyes. "When God closes a door, He opens a window. Have faith, darling."

As the newsroom exploded with social media and highlight leads, the newswoman smiled and noted, "We here at channel six are huge fans of the *All Blacks* and their inspiring captain, Tree Trunks Davies. If you would like to donate to help in the medical expenses, please see the address at the bottom of the screen. The station will be sure that the Davies receive your generous gift."

Suddenly, Rose lost her balance as Robby pushed, nearly kicking her with both of his legs. She landed on the floor, the wind knocked out of her, and it inspired a severe coughing fit. Sitting up, she wiped her eyes and listened to Robby go off on a tirade.

"Shut it off! Shut it off! What the hell is she trying to do? Where the fuck is Ray?" Robby screamed.

"Calm down. Let me get you back into your chair," Rose said, trying to calm him.

But he was disconsolate. "She's never going back to the farm! She swore she'd never wear gum boots again, let alone dodge cow shit in the milking shed. How could she say that? It sounds like we're flat broke! Ray!" As Robby yelled, his movement increased and he worked his body like Rose had never seen since he'd arrived in the hospital. Hearing his name, Ray appeared in the rehab room, panting and out of breath.

"What the hell is going on in here?" Ray gasped.

Rose spoke first as Robby stopped short when he realized what had happened. "The bad news is that it seems Helen Davies is playing the sympathy card. The good news is that we've made a huge breakthrough in Robby's recovery." She pointed to the chair where Robby sat. In his anger, he had the strength and ability to climb into the chair by himself. All of them, including Robby, were stunned.

"Where are the tickets?" Micah barked. "Emily hates to be late."

"Forgive me, sir, but do you think it's really a good idea? Don't you think people will notice? It may be dark in Orchestra Hall during the performance, but don't you think someone might recognize her when the house lights come up for intermission? The balcony's all yours but I think someone might see." Jacob hated to argue with his master, but he loved the siblings and keeping them safe was of the utmost importance. "I know you wish to spoil Miss Emily."

Micah, refreshed from a good sleep in his home soil, had awoken with a clearer head. Surely Jacob was right. Emily's disappearance was still one of Detroit's unsolved mysteries, and as far as he knew the case was still open. "Forgive me, I only mean to cherish my darling sister as she should be cherished. I've neglected her for too many years and her unfortunate state of being is solely my fault."

"Leave it to me, sir. I have the perfect solution."

Within an hour, Jacob had taken Micah and Emily, dressed in black tie attire, to a lovely upper room inside St. Patrick's Church.

"This used to be the sacristy where the priests and altar boys used to change before Mass," Jacob explained. "They renovated and now no one ever comes to this side of the building, especially at night. I grew up in this parish. Father was kind and had this installed for us poorer children. He thought that music should be for everyone. He was a good man." Jacob smiled but it was bitter-sweet. Clearly his mentor had died. Pulling back the curtain from the wall, a small monitor came to life with the flick of the switch. The sound of the audience from the building next door crackled in the speaker. Soon, the stark room was filled with the opening number. Micah placed Emily on an old church pew. He paced as he listened, only stopping to stare out the window.

He spoke to Jacob telepathically so as not to disturb Emily and her concert. "What's that building next door? Show me."

Jacob revealed his mind to his master. While Jacob was subservient and loyal, he wasn't bright beyond a mild tendency towards music. Yet, his minion showed Micah an interesting prospect. He wondered why Micah had never noticed it before. The old Detroit meat packing house was abandoned on the fringe of Towne Center. It was a crumbling gem of disintegration. Micah explored Jacob's mental observations: the grated floors, the upper floors with their observation decks. Tchaikovsky flowed from the speakers, over Emily's corpse and into the shared vision of master and servant. Micah's brain extrapolated as he released Jacob. Moving the remaining equipment and modifying the abandoned warehouse would be simple and would require little effort to accomplish Ruth's plan for *the game*. When the concert was finished, Micah sent Ruth an e-ticket to Detroit.

A spread sheet with bank accounts, stocks and investments glowed before two men sitting in front of a hospital side table.

"She's cleaned out all of the joint accounts. She can't touch your single accounts, though." Ray tried to sound reassuring as he showed Robby the bank details. "Coach called today and asked if everything was okay because she called him at home. She said you were unstable and needed the World Cup bonus to be sent to a new account. He called me to see if you'd gotten worse." There was a knock at the door and Ray went and opened it.

Rose was standing in the doorway, looking meek and small in her sundress. "I wanted to bring this to you," she said. "It's being added to your file. I'm taking a leave of absence. You should know that two men came to see me today. They were doctors working for a law firm. I didn't want to upset you, but today is my last day and I wanted you to know. Your wife is trying to declare you incompetent. The doctors came to interview me because I've spent the most time with you here in rehab."

Robby looked completely spent by Helen's betrayal. He held his breath after asking Rose, "What did you tell them?"

Rose laughed and it inspired a small amount of harsh coughing. Robby idly remembered her coughing before and wondered if she was sick.

Rose smiled brightly and answered, "I told them that you're the most likely candidate I ever had for a complete recovery, and that was due to your excellent mental outlook. Then I gave them the name of a few of the staff who agree with me."

Robby couldn't help himself as he exhaled a huge sigh of relief. Rose turned to leave.

"Wait. Come inside for a moment, will you?" Ray asked her. He stared deep into Robby's eyes as he asked Rose, "What's the likelihood that Robby could be made to stand upright and walk a bit in six weeks?"

"Now come on, Ray!" Robby protested.

Ray ignored him and continued. "Coach also asked if there was anyway they could renew his contract for next year."

Robby knew what Ray was getting at. If he could stand with limited range of walking, he was eligible for Micah's offer in *the game*. And if he were to win, an immortal with superhuman strength sounded like an answer to every prayer.

"If you would have asked me a week ago, I would have said it was impossible," Rose replied. "But with the huge progress Robby's made this week, I'd rethink that outcome."

Rose turned to leave again and Robby decided to take a chance and asked, "Is it terminal?"

Rose stopped mid-step. "Is what?" she feigned misunderstanding.

"My dad coughed like that just before he died of lung cancer. How long have you got?"

Rose didn't say anything for a full minute. When she answered, her voice cracked. "Six months, maybe, if I'm lucky."

"What would you give to survive it? Would you risk everything on something that's likely suicide?" Robby asked.

Chapter 5

Paris was coming to life in mid-March. The boxwood hedges had turned from silver to bright green. The topiaries lining the touristy cafe surrounding the Eiffel Tower gave off a clean, pine scent. It was a sharp contrast to the heavy, luscious aromas drifting over patient patrons of the crepe truck. Fashionably dressed Parisians walked in their trench coats, going about their day unaware that monsters conspired in the apartment above their heads.

Ruth had sent her new king for the vampiric side of *the game* out to find his queen. James wasted no time tracking down Geraldine. He stood on the street just outside her apartment window and listened. She was just waking.

While mortal, Geraldine had little use for the likes of the day, and anything that was of any importance to her happened in the dark. When she answered the door, a wave of surprise washed over her face. Leaving the door open, she invited him in, turning her back and letting him take in her body, draped in nothing more than a thin, gauze shirt from one of her lovers. Her hair was haphazardly arranged in a knot piled on top of her head, and two pins held it precariously in place. It made her neck appear more elongated and her sleek body linear. The pale light from the lamp highlighted her melon-colored lips and deep cheek bones.

Her English was heavy with a thick accent, but grammatically impeccable. "I'm pleased to see that you're still alive after all this time!" she smiled. Tilting her palm towards the table filled with jars, prescription bottles and syringes, she became businesslike. "What's your pleasure?"

"My tastes have, uh, changed," James answered vaguely. He touched her chin and lifted her head ever so slightly to meet his gaze. In his telepathic seduction, he flooded her senses with the smell of roses, the taste of champagne, and a desire for him in her bed that made her cheeks flush.

"I've come for you," he whispered.

To his surprise, she stood up to face him, smiling, but meeting his gaze with a certain determination that most women feared to return.

"You have changed," she remarked. "In so many ways. So tell me, when did you start craving French women over heroin?"

He pressed her further, sitting her down and showing her mind his plans for her body. Her knees parted slightly and she closed her eyes in an attempt to break the spell. "I've met your kind before. Vampires never come into a room without someone dying. Are you here to drink my blood?"

James was impressed to find no trace of fear in her voice. "I'm here to offer you a trade." He forced her to meet his eyes again. He showed Geraldine a life she could only guess at, with her intense beauty and profound knowledge of the human condition. Geraldine was high up in the Parisian drug cartel, climbing the ladder by impressing people far more powerful than James through the years. Geraldine was as lethal as she was attractive and smart.

"You know I never indulge in anything I sell, so why would I take your offer? I don't need an addiction to anything, particularly human blood. I already have money and power. Why do I need you?"

There was a certain detachment to life that the French manipulated in ways like no other culture in the world. One minute they were so in love with life, they were devoting cities to esthetics and beauty. The next minute, they were cold and detached, willing to suffer whatever discomfort in the name of stubborn pride and independence.

"I can give you the one thing no one else can. Time. You can outlive everyone else." He pulled the pins from her top notch with a bit of force to make her take notice. He ran his fingers through her long hair. It smelled of coconut and lavender. "What woman as beautiful as you wants to grow old?"

Geraldine considered James' tempting offer. Vanity was a demon more seductive than any vampire.

"And in exchange?" she asked, brushing away his hand from her hair and examining his chiseled features.

"I want you to seduce a powerful man. I need you to extract every crucial ounce of information you can. He must be bent completely to your will. Agree to this and I'll give you the monopoly of the European black market."

"And if I refuse you?"

"You won't," James whispered, leaning in to kiss her.

The lights of Detroit police cars flashed chaotically a few minutes after a woman reported taking cover at the sound of the gunshot. In the background, the 9-1-1 operator could hear other women as they screamed. A startled baby wailed as it was torn from its early evening nap in the nearby bus station. In the confusion and chaos of gunfire, Riley watched her world in slow motion. Her mind searched the crowd for ways to escape.

There was the old man, leaning against his cane at the streetlamp pole just at the corner of the Detroit Institute of Arts grounds. She could hide behind him but he was a weak shield. The option of attacking the gunman was impossible. She had no weapon. Though she hated to admit it, she was only a girl of twelve. She looked for a police officer, or maybe a bouncer on his way to work at one of the mid-town Detroit clubs. Neither was in sight. That only left one option, according to logic. Driven by her human sense of fight or flight, she found herself staring at the running and tripping feet of the adults who surrounded her, who had been leaving work and heading home when the gunshots rang out.

The words of her father, with his deep voice and thick accent played in her ears. "Sometimes, my girl, it's best to hide your position deep in the throng of the game until it's safe. Sometimes surprise is the best weapon we have and the beginning of any surprise is hiding."

Riley ran behind a large, metal lawn sculpture just beyond the steps of the Detroit Institute of Arts, and waited until it was safe to move.

"Here's the list of future champions." Jeremiah smiled wryly as he slid the paper across the table. Next to each name, he had placed the country of origin. "If you need interpreters, let me know. But I'm sure a man of your vast intelligence has no barriers when it comes to language."

"You flatter me," Cadel laughed, soaking in the praise like a sponge to water. "A *game* of this caliber won't be easy to pull off in this modern time, but I must say I'm impressed, Jeremiah. Resurrecting an old tradition to solve a new world problem is genius, if I do say so myself. Your confidence in your team and your Council may just be what our race needs."

"It's a selfish notion, really," Jeremiah lied. "Many of us long to relive the glory of your last epic victory. With you as our side's game master, how can we lose?" Jeremiah flattered.

"Let's celebrate!" Cadel snapped his fingers and a young woman appeared from nowhere. "My friend has come all the way from America and we must show him how hospitable we Italians are. Do we have anything special in the cellar?"

"Leave it to me, sir," the young woman said and departed.

"It'll just be a moment. You must be starved," Cadel reassured Jeremiah, and pleased to play host to his old friend. He looked back at the list, reviewing it with more scrutiny. "And you're sure these prisoners will comply with my directions? I am, after all, sending some to their death."

"Each will be fitted with headsets and helio-bonds in their uniforms. Those who are non-compliant will find themselves cooked inside their custom-made suit," Jeremiah boasted. "One of our own has perfected the advanced technology in America. It'll be a chance to show what modern innovation can do. I think other Councils with similar offender problems will find it useful."

A few minutes later, Cadel's female assistant arrived with two men, both barely twenty, each holding paint cans in their hands.

"Right this way, gentlemen. The room I spoke of is in here," the young woman said.

The two workers looked around the impeccable room in confusion. Then they began setting up the drop cloths in the far corner. Cadel offered the two men each a glass of wine. Never turning down the chance for a slight delay in working, they agreed. Cadel and Jeremiah toasted the workers, and to each other. But before the wine reached the younger men's lips, the painter closest to Cadel found himself flipped onto the huge mahogany dining table, where Cadel held him down with one hand and plunged his teeth into the man's jugular.

Jeremiah preferred to feed a little differently. Carrying the second painter into the air, he dropped the struggling young man, letting him fall the three stories down from the top of the cathedral ceiling. The painter tried to scream, but all the wind was knocked out of him from the bone-crushing landing. Jeremiah swooped down and picked up the broken human form, and drank from the back of the victim's neck, paralyzing the worker but leaving him alive to preserve the vitality of his blood.

When the two vampires had finished feeding, the young woman appeared again, and began clearing the bodies and the paint supplies.

Cadel sat back in his chair. "The younger generation just doesn't respect the fine art of subtlety." He glanced at the renovation ploy set up by his minion to draw in meals for her master.

"I agree," Jeremiah sighed. "The fact that we need incarceration, rehabilitation and the resurrection of *the game* at all is a sad state of affairs indeed."

"This is a joke, right?" Ruth asked dryly. She stood in the vacant Detroit meat packing house.

"Your lack of vision is really quite staggering," Micah hissed. He waved his hand in the air much like a game show host to a contestant as the curtain revealed a new car. "Close your eyes. Imagine the processing equipment gone." To his surprise, Ruth did in fact close her eyes. "Notice the grated floor, just like you asked for."

"Is there a basement floor below the grates?" Ruth asked.

"Yes. The bottom floor runs the entire length of the building."

"We can feed the insane ones with the spilled human blood from the game," she rationalized. "With proper feedings for several days, we may be able to save some of them. Being a meat packing house, is there an incinerator?"

"No, but it houses an industrialized boiler furnace. Why?"

Ruth walked around slowly, staring up at the immense warehouse lights. "Those that can't be saved with feeding will be disposed of, along with the remains of the human bodies."

"The insane won't go back to the *facility*?" Micah asked, allowing his emotions to shine through his typical reserve.

"Have you a plan to pay for the eternal incarceration of a vampire unable to feed or conceal itself?" she sneered. "We aren't a nursing home for the elderly!"

Micah made a silent vow to himself that when the time was right, he would bring the matter to Jeremiah. He let the matter go and continued with the tour. "There were two separate entrances put in during a foot and mouth scare years ago. You could protect your human audience from the vampire community...or ensnare it. Whichever..." Micah mused.

"We're improving relations, not devouring them."

"Right. We're showing how warm and fuzzy and controllable vampires are by inviting humans to watch them kill other humans," Micah argued.

"Humans see dead people every day in everything from war to video games. But rarely do they see a vampire council make an example of their own by killing them."

Micah stopped arguing. She had a point but he wondered if she could see the potential for it backfiring on her. "As an added bonus, Emily and I checked and the building is for sale, cheap. The airport is only a few minutes away, too. The surrounding metropolitan Detroit area has a variety of flavors to satisfy any of our vampire palates with an added perk. The city is too poor to install the typical security cameras and take the measures most governments consider part of its infrastructure."

"How soon can we place a bid and obtain permits?"

"Emily and Jacob are already looking into it," he said.

"I met your man at the airport but not Emily."

"She's my sister. A lovely cellist and the real jewel of our family," Micah boasted proudly.

"I would love to meet her," Ruth lied. She hated personal ties and despised sentimental gatherings. "When can I?"

"I'm afraid that won't be possible. Emily is leaving to go on tour," Micah replied. He realized in a panic that he had forgotten himself and revealed a vulnerability.

Ruth was both suspicious and indifferent. "Maybe next time then. Let me know when the building is ours. We're down to eight weeks and I don't intend to miss our deadline. The world's most prominent eyes are upon us now."

James ran his tongue along the edge of Geraldine's thigh, making her gasp. He had been listening to her moan as his tongue moved ever closer to her nether region. Beads of sweat ran down her torso and collected into her navel. Soon he heard her begin to beg.

"Please," she whispered.

"Please what? Tell me what you want?"

She lifted her pelvis towards his teasing tongue as she pleaded for more. James was amused. Sometimes she pleaded in English, but as her excitement grew, she forgot herself and it turned to her native French.

"Mon cou," she said, breathlessly pulling James' face from her pelvis.

"Cheri, your neck just will not do," he said. "Your neck is far too beautiful to scar for eternity and will surely give you away." He placed both of his palms firmly on her breasts, lifting them ever so slightly as he inserted himself into her. Geraldine gasped, inhaling and exhaling to the pace James set. As he quickened, he arched her back and pulled her to him. As the two began to climax, he pointed her chest to the ceiling, biting her first just under the right breast, then the left. Traces of her blood trickled down her belly. Just before he finished taking his pleasure in her body, he drew her blood ceremoniously a third time, this time plunging his teeth into the fragile skin of her delicate inner palm. As soon as he drew blood the third time, her body froze and stiffened in agony.

Geraldine's eyes filled with fear and she gripped his throat in her feeble attempt to fight. He laid her constricting body flat on the bed and stroked her hair to reassure her. He listened to her heart as it went from beating hard in the pleasure of his intercourse, to a slowing tempo of the afterglow, to the death throws of a woman slowly dying in the arms of her lethal lover. Once her heart had completely stopped, James lay in bed next to her and waited for the sun to set once more. He knew that when the night blanketed the city in darkness again, he would have a powerful queen by his side.

Chapter 6

Robby's heart felt as if it had fallen to the floor after Rose left. All of the air seemed to leave the room on the trail of her flowing skirt. He had explained Micah's offer to her, though he admitted that he was still grappling with the idea himself. But after discovering that her cancer was terminal, he made the same offer to her. She hadn't reacted angrily like he had when Ray had proposed the idea to him. She hadn't laughed or suggested a CAT scan like she should have. Instead, she walked away, taking every molecule of oxygen out of the room with her. As her perfume lingered, he was left with the dreaded feeling that he would never see her again.

Robby's cell phone rang with a text from Helen. `My attorney has advised me not to contact you, but I just wanted you to know I'm doing all of this because I love you. The talk show money, the book offer and declaring you unfit to manage our finances, is the only way to properly take care of you now. I love you, darling.`

Robby showed Ray the text.

Ray frowned. "She wants you to text back so she can use your written response against you and have you committed."

Robby balled his hands into fists. "It's all for show now, isn't it?" He looked to Ray for confirmation. "The formal announcements to the press, the interviews, the emails to our friends, the meetings with the rugby club, it's all to make it look like she loves me. She's doing what everyone thinks she should do in this situation. She's never been here once to see me since the doctor said I would never play again! She hasn't spent one night here with me!"

Ray had little advice to give Robby. He wanted to comfort him, but there weren't any words.

"Did you get the statement from the doctors?" Robby asked, hoping for some kind of good news.

"That's the bright spot, mate. You've been declared mentally fit as a fiddle thanks to our Rose." Ray smiled, sounding more chipper than he should have.

Robby scowled. He didn't like the sound of 'our' when it came to Rose. His uncomfortable reaction was both surprising and annoying. It left him in a loathing mood as he began to stretch before his leg therapy.

Ray left him to brood.

Walking down the hall so he was out of hearing of Robby's room, he placed a call to Micah. "I'm going to need some help if you want the golden boy. What have you got to sweeten the deal?"

Micah had learned by watching his father. He would sit for hours under the leather-topped table in his father's office, listening. His father made nothing, nor serviced anything. Instead, he just moved money. When money shifted, so did the power in any situation. Micah remembered this as he listened to Ray. He was slowly beginning to take a dislike to the all star manager, but he was necessary in the grand scheme.

"Send me all of their account records," Micah said. "Everything you have from both of them. If Robby signs the contract tonight, I'll make sure his wife's assets are frozen by morning."

Ray was short and curt as he answered, "Fine. You'll have everything I've got within the hour."

"You were hoping for something more lucrative?" Micah mused. "Are you looking to sweeten the deal for Robby or for you?"

"One hour," Ray said and hung up.

Walking all the way to the hospital chapel, Ray found a quiet place where no one could hear him, and made a second call. When the other end of the line was opened, he said quickly, "Meet me at the hotel in twenty minutes."

Rose unlocked the door to her apartment. She threw the mail and her keys onto the side table and dropped down onto her overstuffed couch. Her stomach growled but she ignored it. Eating was pointless, when she thought about it. For hours she simply laid there, staring at the ceiling as thoughts played out like a movie in her mind, utterly vivid in a disjointed collage.

There was Ann's face, a long time medical colleague staring at her from the other side of the desk. Rose wasn't inclined to being a patient. Being a patient required being still and accepting news she didn't want to hear. She watched Ann's lightly-glossed lips form the words *cancer* and *inoperable*. There was some mental vast chasm between the formation of the word and what it meant. Rose blinked, staring at Ann's mouth; part of her thought she was hearing another language.

Lying on the couch, she realized her protective, logical self was shielding her from the devastating news. The mind was strange and wonderful. Logic reasoned that if she didn't know what the words meant, she couldn't be afraid of them, but the wall of logic was turning from stone to thin paper and the dam of watery emotion was soaking and seeping through the fragile wall that protected her from the dark reality. The levy that had held for weeks, as she mechanically prepared paper work and handed off patients, was breaking.

The floodgates finally broke in Rose, and like any flood, it swept away everything in its path. The tidal wave washed over her, breaking the foundations of who she was, how she perceived her world, and her role within it. To fathom dying young was so unfair and wrong that it left her disconsolate. Rose punched the couch, then she threw the morning's cold cup of coffee out onto her small balcony, smashing the cup as it hit the iron bars. She jumped on her treadmill and ran frantically, madly, erratically running nowhere as tears poured down her face.

When the sobbing and the tantrum had rendered her exhausted, she threw herself onto the couch again. She couldn't sleep. Was that right? No, she was afraid to sleep. What if Ann, in all of her kindness and empathy as both doctor and friend, had given her the best case scenario? What if there was less time?

Anger reared its ugly head, but Rose was too tired this time. She wanted to fight but her opponent was incurable. She let the meaning of that word soak into her, deeper and deeper. Ann wanted her to surrender.

No knife could cut out the tumors. No chemical poured into her body could melt the cancer. The monster that devoured her good tissue, drank up the oxygen she breathed, took in the nutrients she ate, turned around and used it to kill her faster every day. The monster inside grew stronger while she weakened. Her only consolation was that in the end, she would take it down with her. When she breathed her last, so too would the monster. If only she could be awake, have some kind of consciousness awarded to her to listen to the monster in its death throws. Rose smiled ever so slightly at the thought of the monster suffering, and her being there to see it.

Like a trickle of hope, as fragile as a seedling in a spring thunderstorm, Rose thought of Robby. Madness took up residency as it replaced surrender or acceptance or anything else that Ann had proposed. She dug her phone out of her therapy bag and dialed the number.

Robby was happy to hear from her but she cut him off in mid-sentence.

"There's a private gym in my apartment complex. Check yourself out of the hospital tonight. Have Ray bring you here. I'll have you standing in a week if it kills both of us. Tell them to send two contracts. I'm in."

"What's wrong? You sounded upset on the phone?" Helen asked, sounding more angry than concerned.

"The accountant didn't offer money," Ray said frantically. "In fact, he's about to separate what's yours and what's Robby's." Ray was emptying the bureau drawers and closet of Helen's hotel room, throwing the contents into two small suitcases.

Helen looked on, calm and cool. "So let him separate them. I'll sue him for whatever does end up on my side."

"He's having your accounts frozen. Pull out just enough to stay out of sight and get the hell out of here."

Helen sat down in the comfortable chair of her hotel suite and watched Ray move from one corner of the room to another.

"Don't just sit there. Get moving, woman! Don't you understand? He'll connect us. He'll figure out that I'm the one who got you all those spots. He hasn't figured it out now, but he will."

Helen remained still. "Why do I care? I have public statements with every major news channel and paper stating my undying devotion to the wellbeing of my husband. The only one who'll look like a traitor is you. I've made sure to send all the receipts of your paychecks, and their inflated amounts as of late, to my accountant. He's ready to leak it to every press agency and sports coverage all over the world. So you see, Ray, I'm not going anywhere."

Rose smoothed out her running jacket and fixed the notch in her ponytail. She stared at her swollen eyes in the mirror and applied a small dollop of concealer. Two days of crying and ignoring her grumbling stomach had made her gaunt and tired looking. She took a deep breath and reassured her reflection, "So an all star rugby player, a major league scout and a vampire walk into your apartment." She laughed at the ludicrous joke. "You can do this," she said. The pep talk was cut short by a knock at the door.

The three familiar men stared at her when she opened the door. Robby wheeled himself in first followed by Ray. Micah stood and waited in the hall.

"Are you coming?" Rose asked.

"That's close enough to an invitation, I suppose," Micah said with a grim smile. Rose turned to close the door and a very strong hand pushed the door back at her. The force of the push back nearly knocked Rose in her weakened state to the floor.

"Forgive me for being late. May I come in?" Ruth asked, opening the door wider to the surprise of Rose.

Micah smiled and welcomed Ruth in over the threshold. Rose looked concerned as she looked at Robby. Upon meeting Ruth, Rose was suddenly afraid. Her instinct was suddenly to run out of the apartment but her protective side wouldn't leave Robby. They all sat down at the small dining room table. As Micah handed out contracts, plane tickets and information packets to Rose and

Robby, Ruth took in her surroundings. Rose watched her do so uncomfortably.

Ruth's eyes met hers. Smiling pompously, Ruth declared, "Simple but tasteful."

Rose looked at her with disdain, "Never underestimate the great things that come from humble beginnings."

In the background, the men were talking logistics and flight schedules to Detroit, but abruptly stopped as the two women began to raise their voices.

"So you intend to become something great in all of this?" Ruth challenged.

"I'm the most powerful piece on the board. Yes, I intend to win," Rose countered.

"*The game* is only won when the pieces work together. Your self-serving attitude might just be the undoing of your king," Ruth warned. She leaned in closer as the three men looked on incredulously. "And remember, it's all about the king in the end. Your power means nothing. If he dies, you all die, and I think I shall truly enjoy watching as Cadel directs his pieces to tear off your limbs before they kill you."

Rose stared back, unflinching.

"Which reminds me," Ruth said. "You two will be given a stipend. You have three weeks to find the rest of your team and your game master. Hopefully your master can control his queen better than the king can," she spat, giving Robby a venomous stare.

Micah shifted in his chair and pulled on his tie. "Ray, I didn't receive any further documentation last night, so I assume the present contract meets your standards?"

"All set," Ray said.

Micah glanced at Robby, who was looking confused, and handed him and Rose each a pen. As soon as the contracts were signed, Ruth was a blur, leaving and closing Rose's apartment door with a slam.

Micah and Ray exhaled but Robby burst into a roaring belly laugh. He leaned over and wrapped his bear-like arms around Rose, and gave her a squeeze. "That was excellent! This game might not be so boring after all!"

Chapter 7

Robby lay on the floor, breathing hard. Beads of sweat ran down his face from his scalp. Rose had doubled his physical therapy sessions. He wondered if she was trying to cure him or kill him at the pace they were keeping. As he lifted weights, she read to him the rules of chess; how the pieces moved and the basics of strategy.

"Why can't we just move ourselves?" Rose protested, looking up from her library book. "I'm not sure how I'll take it, being sent to my death."

Robby stopped and smirked. "A woman who doesn't like to be told what to do."

"I suppose you don't mind?" Rose pressed.

"Being on a team is all about trust. Even if the play seems unlikely, you have to trust that the captain and the coach have made the best play they can." His smile was wildly infectious. "Sometimes an unlikely player will bring the best outcome." As he said it, he pulled himself up on the weight machine, stood on his feet, and let go. Rose threw her book to the floor and placed her hands protectively near Robby, as if forming some invisible force field. Robby laughed and pulled Rose in, hugging her. Neither of them realized but they had both begun to cry.

"Well done, Rose," Robby whispered. "Well done."

From that fateful afternoon, Robby's recovery became unstoppable. Within a week, he was taking short walks with her to her car parked in the street outside her apartment building. Soon, he was able to travel and assemble their much needed team. The deadline for *the game* was drawing closer.

"Where are we headed first?" Robby asked as they got into a cab.

"New York; to the Eastern Chess Championship." She turned to the driver, "To the airport, please," Rose directed.

Geraldine awoke at the precise moment that the Parisian sun was setting. A burning filled her throat and a voracious hunger threw her into consciousness. She had been dreaming wild and terrible dreams that continued to plague her waking mind. She rolled over to find her bed was empty. Her heightened senses searched the apartment for James. She craved him with a carnal lust nearly equal to her thirst for blood. Her body ached inside and out, and she nearly wept with deep desire on every level.

She threw back the covers revealing her naked body in the lamp light. She called out for James, searching the room much like a desperate, caged animal. She could sense him nearby. Why didn't he answer her? She felt her anger growing with the increased agitation. When James stepped into her room from the small balcony, the wind blew in with him. On the wind was the scent of a feast begging for the taking. Naked and famished, Geraldine rushed to the balcony.

Just before her dainty fingertips reached him, James clicked a small, pen-like device, activating her helio-bonds, and Geraldine collapsed to the floor. She screamed and kicked, grabbing at her throat, twisting her hips.

James looked down on her with pity. "I don't have time to put up with the unforgivable antics of a newly-bitten vampire. You're my secret weapon and I'll keep you as such." He took a deep breath and brought his wrist to his mouth. Closing his eyes as if in meditation, he bit hard into his wrist, and immediately offered the blood to Geraldine's perfect lips.

Forgetting the pain of her helio-bonds, Geraldine greedily drank from James. He had gorged during her metamorphosis in order to master his minion. When James felt she had drunk enough, he pulled away from her hungry mouth. Soaked and glistening, blood ran down her plump lips and chin, dripping onto her protruding collar bone. She closed her eyes, basking in the intense feeling of satiated bloodlust.

"Now," James instructed, "we've been instructed to meet the royalty of our opposing team." He grinned. "While Cadel will be eating out of your Lily-white hands, we must ensure to smash the competition. I promise you a delicious meal once we've reached our destination." James traced the blood on her mouth with a finger. Her tongue met his fingertip.

"Remember," he said. "First we put the fear of God into our opponents, then we meet with Cadel. He must desire you above all things. You must become his addiction. Cadel controls *the game*. But you, my darling, will control Cadel."

Geraldine laughed. "You keep me in blood like that and I'll have Cadel to his knees." She sauntered to the bathroom and stared at her blood-covered face. Washing it away with steaming water, she dressed and arranged her golden hair.

James, his heart ever dedicated to Quinn, had to begrudgingly admit that Geraldine was a goddess. Her dress was shear and suggestive of a perfect body, preserved at its peak of perfection thanks to him.

Geraldine watched James and reassured him. "The best way to get a man to want something is by telling him he can see it, but can't have it."

Rose stared at her watch, while Robby ordered them each a beer.

"Maybe he got lost," she said. "I knew we should have met him at his apartment."

"Relax. The guy just won the Eastern Championship last night. He was probably up late celebrating with his mates."

"Adam is Muslim. He doesn't drink," Rose commented bleakly. "And I doubt chess players celebrate like rugby blokes."

Robby lifted his beer and drank deeply. Rose tapped on her cell phone.

"What are you doing?" he asked.

"I'm texting Adam; asking him if he has the directions to the pub that I sent."

"It's his own bloody home town. I think he can figure out how to find his local pub."

Rose texted anyway. She was doubtful that Adam had a clue where the corner pub was. His personality struck her as A-typical, and not someone known for being late to a meeting.

She saw her phone light up and vibrate on the table top. "He wants to meet at his place. He's included the directions," Rose said and stood up, coughing but determined.

Robby grabbed Rose's hand to steady her. "We're going to have to get you to a doctor soon."

She forced a smile and walked to the exit. Robby chugged the rest of his beer and glanced sadly at Rose's untouched glass as he followed her out of the pub.

The walk was slower with Robby still in recovery, but they made their way to Adam's apartment in a short amount of time and rang the bell. There was no answer.

Robby turned the handle and to his surprise, he walked right in. "Adam, mate, where are you?" he hollered, with Rose at his heels.

The two searched the apartment with no sign of Adam. As the wind blew gently through the drapes, Rose stepped out onto the patio while Robby checked the kitchen.

But as soon as he entered the room, he jumped back and his stomach lurched when he looked in the sink, discovering a butcher knife covered in blood. He quickened his step out of the kitchen and ran to the patio. The scene before him threw his mind into overdrive.

Adam was sitting in a wire chair, his shirt soaked in his own blood. His tongue had been either torn or cut out, and was on the table before him, glistening in the moonlight. His hands were cut off at the wrists. He had clearly been sobbing, as dried tear streaks marked his face. At the sight of Robby, he coughed, trying to speak. A spray of saliva and blood splattered across the cement floor. A man and a woman were standing on the edge of the balcony. Robby did a double take. Were they standing or floating?

"I'm sorry that our first meeting has to be so dramatic," James said casually. "It didn't start out that way. The lovely Geraldine and I only stopped in to see if we might enroll Adam in the possibility of doing some consulting work, you know, sort of old school chess master meets new champion. Ruth thought it a lovely idea. Alas, as I was presenting our offer, you two happened to text. Adam explained he was late for a meeting and I could only assume it was with you. He seemed quite keen to join your under-dog cause. That's when things got, well, ugly." James waved his hand like a game show host as if the man bleeding to death was a new washer and dryer. "We started by cutting off his hands to ensure he would never touch a fucking chess piece again." James leapt off the railing gracefully and jerked Adam's head back by the hair, and looked him straight in the eyes. "But I wasn't completely convinced he'd refuse to help you. And you see, there's absolutely no way we can allow you to persuade the newest chess champion onto your side. No hard feelings. It's a mere matter of survival. And speaking of survival, do you want to put the poor boy out of his misery? I mean, I imagine neither of you has ever killed any-one before. We cut out his tongue, so he won't be giving any helpful words of advice on *the game*. All that's left to do is kill him, really. Any takers?"

Robby and Rose stared at James and Geraldine in horror.

"I thought not. You really should get some practice and good-ness knows poor Adam would thank you for it." James grinned evilly.

Robby backed his way to the patio door and put a hand protec-tively over Rose. Geraldine was staring at her hungrily, and it made Robby defensive. James clicked a button in his hand and Geraldine's head jolted backwards, her neckline glowing.

"Never mind then," James said. "Perhaps it's better you saw your own fate in our dear friend here. Geraldine, my lovely, how about that meal I promised you? You must forgive, Geraldine. Her manners are impeccable but she's very thirsty at the moment." Upon hearing this, Adam's eyes bulged with fear and he shook his head no as if to plead for his life.

It took no time for Geraldine to leap nimbly off the railing and onto the patio table. She picked up the severed tongue and licked it, savoring the taste, her eyes rolling back in her head with pleasure. Adam's eyes bulged as she transformed from runway model to monster in a split second. Her mouth gaped open as if it had become unhinged, and before Adam knew it, she lunged in attack, knocking him and the chair to the floor. As Adam lay helplessly on his back, trapped in the chair, her teeth plunged deep into his jugular. Unaccustomed to drinking the blood of others, Geraldine bit down too hard and crushed Adam's windpipe in the process. She drank as much as she could before her victim was dead from lack of oxygen.

Rose began to hyperventilate as Adam's body jerked and twitched in its death throws. His face wore a look of anguish, frozen in death.

James smiled. "Well, I'm glad we've had this first introduction. We really must be going. Ruth is expecting us. See you at *the game*." With that, he took Geraldine's hand and the two leaped together off the railing, gliding effortlessly to the ground several stories below.

When they were gone, Rose felt her knees buckle. Robby pulled her to his chest and they stood trembling together well into the night.

"What have we done?" Rose sobbed. "Adam's dead because of us."

"Didn't you hear what they said?" Robby said. "They were coming for him already. As soon as he won that championship, he was a dead man."

When they felt the two vampires were long gone, they slowly made their way back to their hotel. Once inside, Rose double and triple checked the balcony lock.

Chapter 8

Micah stood at the balcony railing overlooking his handiwork. Four weeks had flown by, but the high wages offered to unemployed skilled union workers had proved itself worth the investment. The old Detroit meat packing plant had been refitted into a proper stadium. The left, upper balcony had been sealed and kept separate for the security of high-end human spectators. Tall glass panels encased half of the stadium seats so as to act as a giant splatter shield. The checkered floor was lined and labeled like a grid, marked with numbers running along the longitude side and letters along the latitude.

The crowning jewel was the holographic screen that hovered over the middle of the stadium-sized chess board. Cameras could zero in on players or illuminate each of the chess masters' individual boards. As an added bonus, Micah's dream child had been a separate set of cameras to highlight the feeding chamber just below the stadium floor. If someone looked closely, the floor of the chess board was grated with holes the size of nickels. When a human was killed by a vampiric player, his or her blood wouldn't go to waste. Instead, a select few deranged and insane from the *facility* could feed. He wasn't sure how it played into Ruth's plan for vampire to human elite PR, but the prominent members of the vampiric community would certainly appreciate his fiscal and nutritional frugality.

In his mind, Micah saw Jeremiah shaking his hand before hundreds of their kind, thanking Micah for saving the downtrodden of their race from insanity-induced by hunger. Those that he saved would owe him their lives for eternity. The possibilities of perpetual benefits were endless. Emily could watch from the closed circuit television he'd rigged in the church sacristy. She would be so proud of him. So happy. A sappy grin crossed his face as the fantasy played out in his mind.

"Patting ourselves on the back, are we?" Ruth's scathing diction ripped through the milky, pleasant sensation of popularity and fame.

Micah wondered to himself how she had come up behind him without detection. His senses were very keen, even when he was fantasizing.

She sauntered over to him, her eyes never leaving his. "Jeremiah has been updating me on all of your progress. You've accomplished quite a bit with the displaced workers." She smiled, leaning in and kissing him, her teeth nipping his bottom lip as she pulled away. "He tells me you really have a way with the people."

Micah smiled back, slightly drunk from her kiss. She leaned in again and this time he pulled her towards him. She ran her fingers through his hair, pulling away at the last minute, she stared at him, her eyes blazing.

Suddenly, there was a loud *click* and then his throat and brain erupted with pain, dropping him to the floor instantly. The pain stopped as quickly as it came and he opened his eyes with trepidation.

Ruth began to shout, "The big question is: *why* am I getting progress reports from Jeremiah? Why? You have a private, direct line to me and yet you choose to align yourself with Jeremiah and the game master."

"No," Micah protested. "That was never my intention. Please."

"I won't have it! You'll see what happens to those who cross me and take power that clearly hasn't been earned."

A thunderous echo rumbled from beneath the stadium floor. Micah tried to get up but was rendered paralyzed by Ruth's heliobond around his neck. There was a creaking of metal hinges and the clattering of wheels and smaller doors. Micah strained to peer through the railing, and down to the floor and the small grates of the giant chess board. He tried to make out the sound that followed next and remember from where he'd heard it before. His eyes stared in disbelief as shadowy figures ran, limped, or were dragged, into the chamber below the stadium floor.

"Consider this quality assurance testing. We need to be sure that the locks and helio-security system you installed will hold and control our lesser-fortunate inmates. It seems unclear as to who wasn't fortunate enough to make the team and who has gone truly mad without the hope of recovery."

Micah didn't see where she was leading the explanation. His helio-bond erupted once again, this time at full strength. He screamed in pain as the tender flesh on his neck began to smolder, then the charge lessened slightly.

"It was so kind of your darling sister and your servant to volunteer to help with our experiment," Ruth continued.

Micah wildly searched the playing field and found a guard carrying Emily to one end of the chess board. With a loud *thud*, a huge spotlight flooded the other end of the board, where Jacob was tied to the floor. Micah grabbed the activated helio-bond in an attempt to tear it off, but Ruth only upped the solar charge. His neck and fingers began to smoke.

Ruth kicked away his hands with her red leather boot. "If you don't stop that kind of nonsense, you'll be too damaged to watch the outcome of the experiment," she cooed. Speaking into her cell phone, she directed the captain in the chamber below the playing field.

"Remember what I told you. Space within the feeding chamber is at a premium. Other Councils have requested a transfer of some of their prisoners. Hence, those who run toward the living blood will be spared. Those who run for the preserved corpse or don't run at all, throw them into the furnace. Are we clear?" A confirmation on the other end of the line was all Ruth needed before hanging up. "Proceed!" she shouted over the railing.

A guard quickly walked from the side line. The sodium lights above illuminated the short, silver dagger in his hand.

When Jacob saw it he began to squirm and scream. "Master, please!" he called out to Micah. "I'm sorry. They took her from me. There were too many. Please, I'll do anything you ask. Anything!" His pleading withered into sobs and Micah closed his eyes, demoralized.

The guard stopped to clip a large gas mask over his face to prevent him from breathing in the scent of fresh blood and thus be riled up himself. As he made his final approach towards Jacob, the young man rolled his hog-tied body away as quickly as he could in defiance. His feeble attempt to escape did nothing more than annoy the guard. Using the rope ends, the guard tied Jacob down to the floor by using the grate holes. Then, he pulled Jacob's head back and made one deep cut to the side of his throat. To slit his throat would have been kinder, but the experiment needed time, and the prisoners needed to find him, so Jacob's final fate was to slowly waste away, drip by drip, as the vampires below fought amongst themselves. At first, all Jacob could hear was his heart beating like a rabbit. It pounded in his ears and made a siren sound in his brain. He couldn't breathe, and yet he couldn't stop breathing so quickly that he felt he might hyperventilate. A hush lay over the stadium as everyone waited, but it was Jacob who heard the noise first: the sound of a thick drop of his blood hitting the concrete floor below. Jacob held his breath and waited.

Micah had every one of his senses divided between the two people he loved most in the world: his sister and Jacob. Micah and Jacob heard the second drop hit the floor below at the same time.

They weren't the only ones.

Dean Sutherland, in his human life, had been a paramedic. He'd lost that human life on a routine domestic call that changed his life forever. He not only heard Jacob's blood hit the floor. He smelled it, too. The aroma was like a distant memory of something from his childhood, something he longed for but had forgotten in the confines of the prison. Dean walked slowly across the floor to the blood drop, and without pride or hesitation, licked the floor like a dog. When Dean looked up, a few more crimson drops fell from above, and for a moment it was as if he were lost in the desert and receiving manna from heaven. But his delight was soon over. A larger, slightly stronger inmate had also smelled Jacob's blood. He knocked Dean's wiry body to the wall and opened his mouth, catching the blood as if he were catching snowflakes on his tongue.

Dean wouldn't give up so easily, however. But the odd confrontation between the two inmates had gotten the attention of some of the others. In seconds, the sharks of the feeding chamber were swarming and fighting for the best chance at another taste. The captain radioed the guard and soon, Jacob found himself at knife point again, but this time it was a merciful slitting of his throat. The captain took notes as the feeding frenzy ensued. The prisoners tore away at one another and climbed on each other to get their gaping jaws around the blood raining down through the grates. Three prisoners had taken the road less traveled and had begun ripping at the clothes protruding through the holes of the grate at the other end of the chamber. As Micah watched Jacob breathe his last, Emily became under attack.

From below, the vampires driven insane with hunger didn't care if they smelled blood or not. They remembered easy prey. Easy prey wore pretty clothes and had long hair, and both of those were just above their heads, and they pulled and tore away at both like ravenous animals. Emily's dried, preserved body crackled under the rough treatment. One of the vampires pulled so hard that he yanked out a fistful of her hair. The other two pulled at the back of her dress, tearing it off. Once her flesh was revealed, they dug into it with their long fingernails. As they ripped Emily's brittle form apart, Micah heard them laughing. Dust from her body filled the air, and soon, all that remained of the corpse was brought to Ruth. As instructed, the guard dropped Emily's bald head before Micah and walked away.

Ruth unlatched the helio-bond around Micah's neck and stared at the trembling, broken vampire at her feet. "Never forget who's really in charge here ever again. You're walking away with your own life intact. Be thankful. Now go and bury what's left of your sister. I'll expect to see you back here tomorrow night."

Ruth left Micah to gather himself and left the building. Once in her car, she dialed a number through her Bluetooth.

"Hello?" a woman's voice said, the voice filled with mock confidence.

"Helen, your husband's financial information has proven quite useful," Ruth said. "Thank you. As I assured you in our last meeting, I pay much better than talk shows. I'll have your payment sent as soon as we hang up."

"And the other promise you made?" Helen dared to ask.

"Eternal youth and beauty takes a far greater investment than just a zip file of debit card transactions, my dear. But continue to prove to me that our relationship should be everlasting, and I'll grant you immortality. I'll be in touch. Just keep your husband's manager on a short leash and we'll all prosper." Ruth hung up without a second thought for the turncoat wife. As she wired the money to Helen's account, she had to laugh. The old human Christian notion was correct after all. When God closed a door, like Micah, *He* opened a window as well, and that window was Robby's adulterous wife.

Chapter 9

Rose blinked repetitively, trying to regain her focus on the room. The fuzzy outlines of odd shapes slowly came into focus, turning moving blobs of shadow and light into people and objects. The glass walls of her Intensive Care Unit room revealed a bustling world of nurses and doctors just outside her door.

There was an unpleasant noise coming from the side of the bed, an underlying base of sound that was louder than the beeping of machines or monitors from above her head. She rolled over to find Robby sound asleep, snoring in a chair at her bedside. The movement of rolling over made her cough and Robby was instantly awake.

Rose tried to speak but her throat was raw and she winced, grabbing at her neck. Robby stared intently at the world outside the glass window, as he handed Rose a cup of ice chips. Rose followed his gaze to find a solitary man, unflinching and unmoving in all of the chaos of an intensive care unit. The man stared back at Robby and Rose.

"He's been watching us since I brought you here," Robby said.

Rose sputtered trying to speak. She managed to get out, "What happened?" It was barely a whisper.

"I woke up to check on you and found you sleeping on a pillow of blood. Since Detroit was our final destination, I brought you here. You've been in intensive care for three days while they gave you antibiotics." Robby explained all of this while looking at the man staring back at him. "I have to find a way to keep you safe while I gather up a team, and for the life of me, I can't figure out how they're tracking us."

Rose looked at him questioningly. Her brain was fighting the drugs and the cancer in order to catch up to the reality she had apparently slept through. She touched his arm and broke Robby's trance with the man outside.

"They arrived at the chess champion's house before us," he said. "They were waiting for us, Rose. Now they know we're here and they're watching. The question is: how?" The sickening realization washed over her that the man outside of her glass room was the hunter and she was the bait.

Dr. Kevin Grey enjoyed his volunteer work. It's what his late wife, Delta, would have wanted him to do. After retiring with tenure at Wayne State, He and his wife had made plans to travel to all of the places he had lectured around the world, but never really had the opportunity to enjoy. Unfortunately, Delta had died before they'd gotten farther than San Francisco.

For the year that followed her funeral, Kevin lived in a bottle of one sort or another, be it their house with the large glass windows of Lathrup Village or the vodka that numbed his heartache. Everywhere he looked, she was there, and for a brief time, her ghost became more than he could take

He considered moving. As he gave a real estate agent the tour of the house, they went into Delta's reading room. It was a place Kevin had kept locked. Everything in that room was hers, and the thought of going inside was enough to make his heart burst from his chest.

Still, there was no explaining that to the agent and so, with trembling hands, Kevin opened the door to a world of memories he had quite literally locked away for a year. He had been right. Being in her reading room had been painful, but not in the way he'd expected. Instead, it was like the bittersweet sensation of returning home after being away for too long.

Her tea cup sat on the small table next to the window. Her chair still had the blanket she had learned to crochet when the children were small. What astounded Kevin most was that he had never really looked at her book collection. A pit formed in the bottom of his stomach as he read the titles for the first time. He first noticed the collection of physics books; all titles he had lectured on. Quietly, she had read up on whatever was taking him away on another junket for the university. The ever-supportive wife of a professor, he never realized she was nearly as well read on his topics as he was.

Excusing himself and showing the realtor out, Kevin spent the next three months reading, taking his meals and sleeping in Delta's reading room. On a hot, July afternoon, while searching through her collection of farm to table cookbooks, an odd little book fell at his feet.

It had no title. It looked like something she might have picked up at a yard sale. But what he found inside was a treasure trove, and he sat in Delta's chair to read it. Her voice filled his mind as he read her neatly-written journal entries.

Somewhere in the small hours of the morning, Kevin found himself falling in love all over again with the wife who had quietly sat idly by as he had made a name for himself and his university. Delta had had plans for her life. The plans were small, but profoundly meaningful. With each book she had collected, three thousand in total according to Kevin's accounts, she had planned to take them and start a library in the cancer ward of the university's research hospital. After a year and three months to the day, Kevin let himself cry holding the words he could read but never hear her say.

It only took a few calls and invitations to the house to convince the Board of Directors. They helped Kevin find the funding. Money was never easy to come by and he felt as though Delta were pulling the strings from some place far more divine than Detroit. As per her plan, Kevin visited the library each week and took stock of what titles were in, what was popular and what needed to be delivered to those too sick to pick up their own copies. The work was satisfying and along the way, Delta sent him to those who needed him most. Her guiding hand was always present.

As he strolled through the bustling cancer ward, Kevin rounded the corner and found that all of the hairs on the back of his neck were standing on end. He was suddenly nauseated from an overwhelming smell, and he grabbed the wall to steady himself. The last time he had felt this way...no, he told himself and dismissed the notion completely. But his mind couldn't let it go. Standing very still, he scanned the nurses' station and the floor. Kevin almost missed him, but then his eyes returned to the man entering a patient's room just two doors down.

Kevin's pulse raced and he checked his watch. The nurses were being briefed as the evening shift handed over patient charts to the midnight shift. No one would have seen the creature enter. No one but a late-night librarian with a past run in with a vampire. Kevin closed his eyes, trying to regain control of his panic. He talked to Delta in his mind, and asked her for help.

Logic told him to wait. There was nothing he could do to stop a vampire once inside the small confines of a hospital room. He would wait and see. As the seconds passed like hours, he listened for the monitors to beep and whistle. Did this one know how to shut down the machines before taking the life of his victim? Why would a vampire feed on a cancer ward? Surely there were more tempting and weaker targets in geriatrics or the ER.

Kevin tried to shut out the memories of his own unpleasant experience with the undead. Goosebumps ran down his back and he wrapped his arms around himself to keep from shivering. Movement was near the room and Kevin stepped back into the closest room, waiting for the half-man, half-monster to leave. When he was sure the elevators had taken the vampire elsewhere, he made his way cautiously to the patient's room and peeked in. A man and woman were sitting on the bed, clearly shaken. The woman was in tears.

Kevin entered the room and stopped at the door. "Good evening. My name is Dr. Kevin Grey. If your friend returns, I feel you might not be so lucky to survive a second time," Kevin said sternly. "I can't help you until dawn breaks. I'll be back for the day shift. If you're both still here, be prepared to check yourself out. Pay with cash. Leave all of your credit cards and identification here. If you've had a visit, you want to be sure to discard any means of tracking. Do you understand?" Robby and Rose stared at Kevin incredulously and then nodded their heads that they understood. Kevin's eyes softened. "It's my dearest hope to see you in the morning. Until then, I suggest you pray."

"Pray? What the bloody hell for? Are you some kind of bible thumper?" Robby was defensive and stood up, ready to throw Kevin out of the room.

Kevin pulled out a crucifix he wore around his neck. "I don't have time to explain right now. Let's just say one of these saved me in a meeting quite similar to the one you just had. It would seem to me, surrounding yourself in a room filled with similar objects, would be helpful. You may not believe in them, but your new friend most certainly does."

Rose pulled off her covers as if she didn't need any further convincing. Robby hesitated. He stared at Kevin, scrutinizing him, sizing him up as a man. There wasn't much time and it wasn't clear who they could trust and whom they couldn't.

Kevin broke the staring contest. "Where are you staying?"

Robby chose his answer carefully. "In a hotel nearby."

"You've been followed. Don't go back there. Not until we've had a chance to talk."

Robby finally shook his head in concession. "Where might I find a wheelchair, mate?"

Cadel was clearly irritable by the way he called for his assistant. He was hollering even before she had made it into the room.

"Have you any idea why they chose this godforsaken city?" It wasn't a question she was meant to answer and she knew it. "I mean, where is the beauty?"

Her petite face gave the impression that her eyes were larger than they were, making her look younger and more alluring. She smiled daintily. "Perhaps, sir, the real beauty is in the macabre of the city. I mean, not everything that's beautiful is perfect, smooth or delicate." She stood before him and dared graze her finger gently over his gnarled hand. "Sometimes the things that are dark and decayed are the most attractive."

Cadel was suddenly reminded of why, above all, he had chosen her to be by his side. One day soon, he would have to turn her. Clearly she had earned the right. He knew all too well that as soon as he gave his faithful servant her heart's desire, she would surely leave his company. Selfishly, he prolonged the inevitable.

"How did your study go, sir?"

"It was interesting. After observing the pair for a long time, I can't decide if they're clever or truly mad. Introducing myself was pointless as well. Until we know who their game master is, I won't know how much influence they have over him. The royal human couple is truly a mystery not so easily analyzed in one night, I'm afraid." A bell chimed, a notice that it was ten minutes until sunrise. "But alas, there are only so many hours in a night."

"I've prepared your coffin, sir. The soil from home arrived yesterday and I've prepared your place to rest."

"Good girl. You're a faithful and humble servant. When we return home, I think we'll celebrate your turning. What do you think?"

"Really, sir? Nothing would make me happier!"

"Make the arrangements. You've earned your place in the eternal night. I won't have my darling Maria turned in this filth and decay. Your coming out will be in the splendor of Italy. Now with that I bid you good day."

Rose was doing her best to kneel in the chapel, but every part of her body was tense and on alert. She was on the cusp of breaking down and focused on breathing to keep herself in check. Robby, on the other hand, stood like a sentry near the door with his back to the wall and his gaze scanning the chapel for any movement. His biceps bulged with his arms folded cross his broad chest, making him look as formidable as humanly possible. That was the problem, he thought to himself. *Humanly* was definitely a disadvantage at this point in the game.

In the ambient lighting and candle flame, shadows became exaggerated. Each flicker of flame or unfamiliar sound made Rose look to Robby as if asking where they would run to or how they would fight. When she considered her own defense, an epiphany, divine or neural, came to her and she slowly stood. Robby was instantly alarmed, but Rose flashed him a wildly-infectious smile. She made her way to the altar near the baptismal font and there, just like the church of her childhood, sat a bowl of small plastic vials. A small, handwritten note stated, "For the sick or homebound."

Rose imagined that the author of the note had never envisioned a pesky vampire problem in the humble hospital chapel. Still, in her heart, she knew her cause was just, if not unusual. One by one, Rose filled a dozen small vials with blessed holy water and put them in the pocket of her hospital scrubs. Robby looked on and joined her in her smile when she returned to her seat. "Bloody clever," he whispered.

Soon, sunlight came streaming through the chapel windows and Robby began to pace. He wasn't sure if he could trust Kevin. Surely the ward would notice Rose was missing from her room and all the while, the ability to hide was growing more and more difficult. As his patience wore threadbare, the door of the chapel cracked open and Kevin peeked in. "Ready?" he asked.

Rose got into her wheelchair and Kevin, with his security badge and lanyard, walked slowly and confidently to the elevators. No one paid them any notice. Taking the service elevators to the garage, the trio got into Kevin's car and were away quickly. The drive to Lathrup Village was calm, heading northbound, the traffic heading in the opposite direction.

At his home, Kevin settled his two guests in Delta's room and offered Rose some of his wife's clothing.

When everyone was cleaned up and having coffee, Kevin decided he had waited long enough. "I know you must be tired and on edge," he said. "Since I know exactly how you feel, let me answer the question that both of you must obviously be asking yourselves. I knew the man in your room to be a vampire by his, well, smell." Kevin waited a few moments for his opening statement to sink in. As a professor, he had often opened his lectures with something to grab his audience's attention. This was no different.

"Think about it. It's the smell of decay and rotting things. I was introduced to that smell many years ago at my university, just next to the hospital. I was staying late, grading papers in my office, when that same smell permeated the entire room. It grew so strong that I felt sick.

"I stood to open my door and run to the men's room when, from above me, the door slammed itself. I looked up and there, on the ceiling, was something not even my nightmares could produce. One of my students, a young and brilliant man, was holding the body of dead girl. The murder was fresh as her blood dripped down onto my scalp. His face was contorted, and I could just barely make out his identity. When he spoke, I confirmed it.

"Let me say that this young man, while brilliant, gave far more credence and imagination to the field of physics than is proper. The things he expected from science kept him from being objective. I'd suggested to him that he leave the department and study something more practical like accounting. When he could be more logical in his approach, I'd re-admit him to the physics department. Hence, this brilliant, wild visionary hovered above my head with murder literally in his hands and death across his face.

"I invited him to sit down. He laid the girl on my desk as if there were a chance of reviving her. Sobbing, he confessed to me that he'd only recently been bitten and awoke in his undead state.

He was starving and burning to feed when he awoke at sunset. Unsure of where to go and without guidance, he opened his window, letting his instincts guide him. Just before he was about to descend, a knock came at his bedroom door. His sister, Emily, had come in to check on him. The scent of her sweet blood consumed him at that moment and he attacked and killed her within seconds.

"Overwhelmed with regret, he recalled a lecture I'd given on time and the mathematical ability for one to move forwards and backwards according to String Theory. I agreed that the theory was correct. I also knew my life was on the line in what I might say in the next few minutes that followed.

"Being a seasoned lecturer, I began to filibuster about dimensions, alternate earths and the strong nuclear bond, praying, much like you two, I imagine today, for the dawn to come. Just as the sky was turning black to gray, a hint of light reflected off of the crucifix around my neck. My window suddenly flew open and vampire and victim vanished. I lived in fear of my life for months that followed. I can only imagine that the police investigation, the high profile of his wealthy family, and the news cameras that I welcomed in front of my house, waiting for my comment or interview, kept him away."

A quiet knock came at the door, making Rose jump. "Come in, come in. Rose, Robby, this is Riley," Kevin said. She arrived here just the other day. Riley is here taking art classes at the Art Institute while her father is back home playing in a large chess tournament. Riley's father and I are research partners."

"He won, too!" Riley beamed. "But I thought he would be back by now." Her expression looked very mature and worried for a twelve-year-old.

Kevin laughed. "You know your father. He's lost track of time, thinking about how he might have beaten his opponent faster and more gracefully. Now, until we hear from him, Mrs. Englewood has made some cookies. If you're done with your treatment today, why don't you go see how many you can sneak for all of us?"

Riley giggled and left the study.

Robby blanched and Rose buckled, her heads resting in her hands.

"Now," Robby declared, "it's time for us to tell you our story. But before I start, I'm going to need something stronger than coffee."

Chapter 10

Micah lay on the velvet sofa in the music room, staring at Emily's bald head that sat like a music icon on the grand piano. Between sobs, he spoke to her. "I just can't. I tried. I dug the hole outside like she said. I dug a grave for you under the cherry tree that blossomed every year on your birthday. But I can't bring myself to do it." Micah erupted into a fit of hysterics.

"Of course you can't bury me under the cherry tree. I deserve better than that!" Emily protested. Micah jerked his head up from the tear-soaked pillow, his eyes wild. "I'm one of Detroit's own, one of the best cello players this city has ever seen. You can't just bury me under some tree in the rich suburbs. I won't lie in mud of an unmarked grave," Emily warned, angry and spiteful.

Micah slid off the sofa like an invertebrate. He moved his spineless body, oozing from the couch to the floor. There, in prostration to his iconic Emily, he begged her, "What should I do? How can I earn your forgiveness?"

There was a long silence in the room. A gentle breeze swept through the open windows. Building momentum, it ruffled the curtains and knocked over a free-standing picture of Emily and Micah's parents off the side table. Suddenly, each window slammed shut and curtains snapped closed. As if orchestrated, the world was shut out one pane at a time; the lights flickered and went out. Micah was left in the darkness with Emily's head staring at him from the piano. Electricity filled the room. The chandelier hanging from the ceiling began to sway, the moonlight sparkling off its prisms. Soot from the fireplace was caught in the wind that mysteriously resided within the house. From the ash and soot, a wind devil appeared.

The tunnel of spinning ash first formed her long, slender legs, then her maiden silhouette, and then her slender, toned arms and fingers. The headless wind tunnel of feminine curvature walked over to the piano and gracefully placed Emily's head on its shoulders much like a queen bestowing a crown upon her head. Kindling from the fireplace formed her makeshift hair. Emily was a composition of all things that remained. Beyond fire, beyond embalming, beyond corpus desecration, she remained. The queen of remains stood before Micah and gave her brother her one and only royal command. As she spoke, her voice echoed off the plaster walls and tile floor. The sheer volume traveled through Micah in waves, stirring him a way that could change lead to gold. It was both a scream and a whisper all at once, and it was simple. "Avenge me! Avenge me, brother. Make them all suffer the way that you have suffered. You know what to do. It's what you've always wanted to do since the night you killed me. Do it. Do it for me." Emily towered over Micah.

He dared lift his eyes to her, squinting in the brutal wind of her form, specks of dirt and debris whipping at his face. She was both terrifying and beautiful. As her eyes blazed, her incarnation grew into rage and the wind pushed Micah backwards. Her voice exploded like metal hitting concrete. "Destroy them!"

With her final command delivered, the wind halted as quickly as it came. Micah stared, trembling, as he lay in the relative safety beside the claw-foot sofa. Emily was stripped of her royal remains, and was once again a severed head that fell to the floor. Micah lay behind the sofa trembling and staring at Emily's face. She was right. He did know what to do. Micah crawled out from his hiding place and picked up Emily. He placed her head on the scroll of her upright cello so he might see her face to face.

The shape, while slightly bottom heavy, was feminine and curvy. It suited Emily. For a second, Micah wondered if Emily, when alive, might have preferred this version of herself; her passion for the cello infused with her mind and face. He smiled at her. "I'll make it all right again, my darling," Micah vowed. "There's no time to waste."

Helen's phone vibrated. It was the fourth text from Ruth she'd received that morning. Her pulse quickened at the sight of the number flashing across the screen.

Extracting information from Ray was becoming more and more of a challenge. Helen scolded herself for losing control of a situation that was quickly spinning out of control. She looked at herself in the mirror and took a deep breath, smoothing out the creases in her short, silk nightie. She double and triple checked the champagne glasses, committing to memory which one was which. To her relief, Ray's familiar knock came at the door. Helen greeted him with her most seductive smile.

"Well, this is a pleasant surprise," Ray beamed as he looked her up and down. She sauntered to the mini-bar and he trailed closely behind her, nearly forgetting to close the hotel door.

"I've filed my divorce papers, claiming Robby mentally and physically incompetent," she said. "I thought we should celebrate. Now it can be just me and you." Sipping her champagne, she handed Ray his glass from the other side of the bar. "Hasn't that been your plan all along, Ray?" Helen's heart sank as Ray set his glass down without taking a sip.

He rushed to her and kissed her hard. "Let me show you what my plan has been for some time now." He moved quickly, years of wanting his client's wife igniting his desire. At first, the notion seemed romantic as Ray guided her out onto the balcony. Helen was thankful that the night had fallen so no one could see her outside in lingerie. Pushing aside her insecurities, she tried talking to Ray, but to no avail. Her mind raced in the confusion of his forcefulness as he pushed her to the balcony edge. She was gripping the metal railing, her head looking down at several stories below. He pushed her panties to the side. She tried to turn around but his body pressed and held her over the railing. She was suddenly afraid. Would he let her fall?

A man taking back control, Ray plunged himself into her, bending her over the hotel railing. In every way, Helen felt exposed and at his mercy. All she could do was hold on for her life. She listened to him puff and grunt as he thrust deeply, and each time Helen tightened her grip on the railing. She focused on breathing, his weight and the angle she was in crushing her ribs and diaphragm. When he had finally finished, she felt his body weight leave her. She took a shaky deep breath and held back the floodgate of tears that threatened to make her look weaker to Ray than was her plan.

As Ray zipped his fly and strolled off to the bathroom, a deep ache for Robby and all of his gentleness formed inside of Helen. But she hardened that place within her and made her way to the mini-bar. Adding an extra tablet to the already-laced champagne, she swirled the bubbles in his glass until the pill had dissolved. Any fear she may have had of overdosing him was long gone. Helen clicked the recording app on her phone for good measure as she bit back another wave of tears.

Handing him his glass as he returned, they toasted, and Helen watched Ray down his entire glass in one large gulp.

Feeling very satisfied in his manhood, he plopped down on the bed and laughed. It was clear the alcohol and drugs were taking an immediate effect.

"So let me get this straight," he said. "I'm the only one with access to his bank account. I'm the only one who knows where he is now." He paused for dramatic effect. "His wife is divorcing him so she can be with me. Oh yeah, and while the courts figure out if he's sane or crazy, I'm fucking his wife, too. It's good to be the manager."

Helen could hear his words begin to slur. She regretted adding the extra drugs. Pouring him another glass, she invited him to sit up.

"So, where is my royal husband?" Helen inquired.

"Why do you care?" Ray sneered.

Her mind raced. "The sooner they serve him his summons to court, the sooner I win all of his money, and the sooner we live happily ever after." She ran her fingers through his tussled hair as he sat in hazy deliberation.

"He's already at the match site," Ray said. "He's checked himself into some hotel in downtown Detroit. I can't see how on earth he'll have sorted anything resembling a team, but he's there already. Maybe he is crazy. It doesn't matter. I've tracked all of his transactions. He hasn't even bought room service. I thought by now he would be shopping for superhero suits or something." Ray yawned. "It doesn't matter. We don't need him anymore." His eyes rolled back in his head and he passed out.

Helen shut off the recording, sent it in a text to Ruth, and waited.

Maria tapped her fingers anxiously as she waited the final moments for sunset. Summer was in its glory. As the days grew longer, so did her longing to report on the ever-growing activities of the household and *the game*. James and his queen had arrived in a dark car. She was honored to meet the royals but suddenly afraid, too. Geraldine's stare made Maria feel more and more like a meal. If she could have, Maria would have run to Cadel and jumped in his coffin. Thankfully, Cadel arrived in the dining room a few seconds later.

"I sense your urgency, my dear," he said. "I came as quickly as I could. What is it my girl?"

"The royal couple just arrived," Maria explained. "I wasn't expecting them and I don't have a proper stock in the cellar for entertaining." She was clearly worried; Cadel found it endearing.

"Don't worry. I have much to discuss with them. While we're busy, make whatever necessary arrangements for a proper feeding before dawn. The royal couple is here, so spare no expense," he instructed.

"Yes, sir. I'll show them in to see you and then leave right away. Leave it to me." Maria smiled, thrilled at the chance to lavish her master with a feast. As soon as Geraldine and James made their way to the dining room, Maria grabbed her keys.

"Maria, dear!" Cadel called. She felt her heart sink but she ran to him anyways, avoiding eye contact with Geraldine. "Forgive me, but the entire team for our side will be assembling and meeting for the first time tonight. Can you handle the additional load?"

"Absolutely," Maria smiled.

"If anyone can pull it off at the spur of the moment, you can. See you soon," Cadel reassured.

Thrilled to be free from the death stare of the new queen, Maria ran to the car and drove off. She did a web search from her cell phone and soon landed on the directory listing, then she made the call. "Hello yes, it would appear that my casting call is a bit thin tonight. I know this is last minute, but could I book models and actors for a very large, very private party taking place just after midnight in my Royal Oak home?"

The woman on the other end of the line gave a doubtful answer followed by an exaggerated price for such short notice.

"I assume these people will be of the highest quality and of the utmost discretion, correct?" As Maria figured, the price went up on the other end of the line. "Excellent. What was your name? I have my credit card ready."

With one hundred of Detroit's most beautiful and unknown booked to attend the party, Maria drove to the Eastern Market. The bustling crowds made her homesick for Italy. But Detroit had its own feel, with the barbecue chicken and ribs smoldering over hot coals in makeshift grills cut and welded together from leftover steel oil drums. Rap music, reggae and Motown blared in opposite corners of the market. Within an hour, Maria had hired a chef and help, purchased enough raw ingredients to feed an army, and over twenty cases of wine. She gave her small, newly-hired staff the address and had a garden party complete with candlelight, and a gourmet spread prepared just in time for the human guests to arrive.

The sun was set to rise at 5:09 a.m. She knocked on the dining room door and entered. Cadel looked at her fondly, admiring her little black dress and her soft wavy hair. Simple but elegant. The room was full of newly-arrived vampires and all their eyes were on her. She nodded to Cadel to confirm everything was ready. He entered her mind and suggested she make the announcement instead of him.

Maria took a deep breath, "If you'll forgive the interruption, a feast has been prepared in your honor and is waiting in the garden."

The team and its royal couple joined the beautiful people of Detroit under the night sky. Model wannabes traded in their beer and whiskey and sipped Pinot Noir instead, trying to sound sophisticated as they networked.

Maria sent her thoughts to Cadel as she looked on at the mingling guests. "I'm afraid the queen doesn't like me. Is it not a party fit for royalty?"

Cadel made his way over to her and wrapped his arms around her protectively in a rare public display of affection. He replied in her mind, "You've done splendidly. The queen will grow to love you as I do. You'll see."

From a corner of the garden, James whispered to Geraldine, "Don't forget that you're here for one reason only. I'd have thought with your skills that you'd have already been in his bed."

Geraldine sipped her wine, staring daggers at Maria. "You can't tempt a man who has no hunger."

James took the glass from Geraldine and smiled, "But you could console a bereaving man's heart."

"I suppose he can't protect her forever."

James held Geraldine's wrist hard as he returned the wine to her. "You don't have forever. You have two nights. I'm the king and if my present queen doesn't suit me, I think Maria might wear royalty just as well if not better. Find a way, or find yourself strapped in a convertible with helio-bonds under the noon sun."

Cadel clinked his glass and the garden grew silent. "Thank you all for coming. The sun will rise in a little over an hour. I suggest everyone enjoy the lovely meal Maria has prepared before the morning is upon us." He raised his glass in a toast. "To *the game*." Everyone raised their glasses, half of the guests unaware what they were toasting. James and Geraldine watched as Cadel led Maria indoors. It was the last they were to see of the game master for the night.

Instead, the royal couple each grabbed the closest victims. James gripped a well-dressed young man in a suit. With one fingernail, he ripped open the man's soft chest tissue and drank from him like a fountain. Women began to scream and the sound of wine glasses hitting the stone patio filled the garden.

A nimble girl, for fear of being trampled, climbed up the courtyard tree. Geraldine was angry and needed a particularly interesting challenge in which to relieve her frustrations. Leaping like a leopard, she landed on a branch just above the girl. There was a scream and crunch as Geraldine bit through the girl's skull.

With the king and queen setting precedent, the chase was on for the rest of their team. Convicted vampires, deprived of fresh blood in the *facility*, gave into the bloodlust. Tearing at whatever human flesh they could find, they gorged on the fleeing human guests.

As the sun rose, the lawn of Cadel's vacation home garden had changed from green to blood red.

Chapter 11

"Thank you, Kevin. Having the wake here really helped Riley," Sarah smiled, holding back tears. "You two really were a great research team."

Kevin nodded. "Your daughter is welcome anytime," he managed to say without tears. "Where is Riley? I'd like to tell her a proper goodbye."

Rose was serving tea to guests in the living room. Kevin peered at her from around the corner. "Have you seen Riley?"

"She's in the garden playing chess."

Riley playing chess was not at all surprising. She had been playing every night with her father since she was three. Riley playing chess must have been a comfort to her, and God bless the soul who sat patiently across from her and took a guaranteed beating. It never occurred to Kevin to think it odd that Riley was playing chess outside, her opponent unable to enter the home until the owner invited him in. He also didn't think to find it odd that a girl had no qualms playing in the garden at night, in the dark.

As Kevin strolled into the garden to collect Riley, he took in the light scent of Delta's roses. Soon, his feet were carrying him faster to the candlelit patio. As he tried to dismiss the next smell that permeated his senses, his instincts kicked into overdrive and his only thought was to protect Riley.

"Uncle Kevin!" Riley beamed as he reached the patio.

"Riley, your mother is looking for you. It's time to go," Kevin said sternly.

"Okay, I'm almost done with the game."

"No! Right now. Your mother's very tired."

Riley looked both surprised and hurt at Kevin's tone. As the man with his back to Kevin turned around, Kevin gasped. His tough demeanor melted away, fear taking hold of him. Kevin went to Riley and hugged her as tears ran down her face. "I didn't mean to you yell at you, Riley," he whispered. He stood, picking her up as she clung to Kevin like a little girl to her father. "I'll arrange it with your mother. You can come here and play a game tomorrow night."

Riley picked her head up and a slight smile crossed her exhausted face. "Promise?"

"Promise," he assured her. "Now, run inside and find your mother. She's waiting."

When Riley was safely away, Kevin turned to Micah. Kevin was furious. Pounding his fist on the table, he knocked all the chess pieces over, some toppling to the patio floor. "How dare you come here! How dare you talk to her! Her father..." Micah cut Kevin off.

"I know all about what's happened. I also know the likelihood of you listening to me and trusting what I might have to offer is small to nil. Still, I'm the best option for you and the ones you're hiding."

"You're my worst nightmare," Kevin said, shaking with emotion.

"Sometimes our worst option is still the best one when you look at the larger picture." Micah paused, sensing someone else in the garden. "And you've run out of time and options haven't you, Tree Trunks?"

Robby stepped into the candlelight. "Sorry, Kevin, I got worried when you didn't come back inside."

Micah clicked his tongue in disapproval at Robby. "You may be king for the human side, but right now, you're the king of forfeit without a full team. If you read the fine print, I'm sure your manager never pointed out that a forfeit means instant and immediate death."

Robby looked to Kevin, who shook his head no. But Robby continued to stare at him. They both knew whatever Micah had to offer had to be considered.

When Helen awoke, her mind searched for something familiar. The light, the sounds, and even her own body felt unfamiliar to her. She ached when she tried to sit up. The floor beneath her was cold and hard.

"Hello?" she called out into the darkness. There was no reply. As she strained to stand upright, the ceiling, completely invisible to her in the darkness, collided with the top of her skull. She crumpled to her knees, tears pooling in her eyes as nausea churned in her stomach.

She listened for a long while. How long, she didn't know. With no light, no sound, and no one to ask, eternity could have been five minutes, five hours, or five days. She tried counting. Every time she made it at an even pace to sixty, she raised a finger. Ten minutes, twenty minutes, thirty. The numbers lulled her back to sleep. Or at least she thought so. When sleeping and waking were both swirled in a sea of sensory deprivation, a person's dreams become reality.

Helen dreamed that she heard a woman's voice. Then, a sliver of yellow light shined inside, blinding her. Two tall mugs were slid on a gray tray. Without hesitation, she reached for one and drank it greedily. The second glass tasted the same.

This dream persisted every day until Helen lost track of the days.

Micah arrived at sunset the following evening.

Kevin peered through the curtains as he deliberated.

"Did you decide to invite him in and listen or should Robby and I go out into the garden?" Rose asked.

"I know the man who's with him," Kevin said. "I'm afraid that I'm a creature of habit and far more human than I care to admit. My curiosity demands I open the door and Micah knows it."

The sun was still in its final death throws but Micah was anxious to get started. As he stood at Kevin's threshold, a light smoke pillowed from his exposed neck and hands from the last rays of sunlight. Kevin opened the door. He stared at both of them. "George, the only reason I'm letting you in my house is because my wife said you were the most decent human being on the planet, and I never second- guess my wife's judge of character. That being said..." Kevin held up a large wooden cross and looked at each man in turn. "I won't hesitate to use this. Are we clear?"

Micah and George nodded yes and Kevin invited them in.

With George beside him, the smoke rose from Micah's collar, leaving a wispy trail as he and George made their way to the kitchen table. Kevin thought how Delta had always said that the kitchen table was where the messy stuff happened, and it was the easiest place to clean up. Rose and Robby were waiting nervously.

Kevin, nervous as well, and openly disapproving of Micah in his home asked, "Before we get started, I want to know what's in this for you? Why help build a team aimed at defeating and killing your own kind?"

"I have my reasons," Micah answered vaguely at first. Then he added, "But the reasons will see me through to your win or my death, whichever comes first."

There was something in Micah's absolute resolve that made Kevin believe him. He didn't want to trust his former student. Somehow, Delta had a hand in all of it and her spirit told Kevin to trust in the most unbelievable of creatures.

George extended his hand to both Rose and Robby. "I'm George Halls."

Rose stared at the burns on Micah's hands, feeling uncomfortable as she watched the last few seconds of twilight. With the recent death fresh in her mind, *the game* seemed more real and far deadlier than the last time she had sat at a table across from Micah.

"This is one of your rooks," Micah announced. "His counterpart will be arriving in an hour with a few others willing to play *the game*."

"*The game* has been explained to you?" Rose asked George with a certain amount of doubt in her voice. Clearly, he was a healthy man, probably in his mid-forties. She wondered if he had been tricked into committing himself under false pretenses.

"I'm fully aware of the life and death stakes and am willing to risk them," George answered keenly.

"My God, why?" Kevin asked.

George gave a half-smile and asked for a beer. Robby grinned, immediately joining in.

"Don't drink that," Micah protested. "Vampires are attracted to flesh made tender and blood thickened by beer."

George and Robby looked at each other and began to laugh at the macabre of the situation.

"In that case…" George jabbed Robby. "We better make those doubles."

As Kevin poured out the beers, George explained, "As Kevin can attest, I've dedicated my life to the research of gene therapy, particularly the gene responsible for Alzheimer's disease. I'm forty-five now. I have at least ten years before I can publish and another ten years before my gene therapy treatment will be eligible for human trials. That takes me to sixty-five." He paused and took a large gulp of his beer, giving Micah a sideways glance as he did so. "When my father's Alzheimer's reached a point where he could no longer live alone, he was sixty-two. By the time he was sixty-five, he didn't know if he should eat the hamburger or the round plate it was on. Two months ago, my tests came back positive. I have the gene marker for Alzheimer's as well. By the time I reach a point where I can save the world from literally losing its mind, the chances are high the same disease will have already rendered me unable to dress myself, let alone lecture for funding." George stood up and began to pace as if he were working out the logistics in his head. "But if I were immortal…" He looked at Kevin directly. "Think of all of the lives we could save and the research we could do, Kevin. Think of it. Never getting tired, never having to take a break, save to close the curtains to block out the sun. In a hundred years we could eradicate cancer. In two hundred years, we could wipe AIDS off the planet." George was rather convincing. Even Rose could see the positive aspects if they won.

"What about the lives you'll take, feasting on blood to keep you alive during those two hundred years?" Kevin countered.

"Dr. Kevorkian changed my outlook on the right to die. You know that argument won't hold water with me," George argued. "Those we can't save, we put out of their misery. You won't convince me otherwise."

"Nor me," a woman said, newly arrived, making Rose jump.

"This is Eleanor, my assistant," George said. "She overheard Micah and I talking late last night and has signed on for the same reasons."

"Signed on?" Kevin asked.

"Contracts and all," Eleanor confirmed.

"Your knights and bishops arrive in a few hours. It's the expendables that I have to find next and those are never very easy," Micah sighed.

"Expendables?" Robby asked.

"I imagine you're referring to the players who will be the pawns, the foot soldiers on the front line, so to speak," Rose confirmed, sadly.

"Yes, but I have a lead on those," Micah announced boastfully. "By tomorrow night, the team will be complete." He clapped his hands and rubbed them together with a dark sort of anticipation.

"Then we'll have everyone to play the bloody game," Robby pointed out.

"On the contrary, you have someone trained by the best that has never played in the chess world, and hence is a complete unknown to Cadel. That's your ace in the hole."

"Who is it?" Kevin asked.

"The only person who has the most right to play this game at all." He glared at Kevin. "The one person who deserves her chance to win for mere vengeance alone. Riley is your game master, and you, my dear professor, will be her protector."

Chapter 12

Micah handed Sgt. Acres an envelope of cash.

Acres put his Marlboro to his lips and yellowing teeth, freeing his fingers to thumb through the bills. "You say you want the winners," he asked.

"That's right," Micah confirmed.

"I'd promised the city council some stats on their rehabilitation program."

Micah smiled. He opened his satchel and handed Acres two files. "Here's an analysis of repeat crime offenders, reintroduction to work program success rates, and quarterly reports of tax savings for your correctional facility for this year."

Acres stared at Micah, unable to fathom where on earth the strange man might have come up with so much fabricated data. He opened his mouth and then closed it again. He didn't want to know and he didn't really care. Micah paid better than the city council, and while the city was broke, the man before him clearly was good for the milking.

"We've held five games so far. The sixth one is about to start and the last two will be done by tomorrow morning," Acres said.

"I'll send a van for the winners tomorrow night. Agreed?" Micah confirmed.

"Sure you don't want the losers?" Acres pressed. If he could sell the losers to Micah, the city would still pay the small sum to fund the rehabilitation for the winners.

"No. I need the winners. I need the ones who can stay calm under pressure. Besides, I'd like to think that the winners will know when they're facing their death."

Acres stared at the vampire. He deliberated. He thought he was selling off the dregs of the city to some sex trade or work camp. This guy had balls, openly speaking about killing them off. Acres respected that.

"Just tell the city that none of the first batch of winners made it through rehabilitation," Micah said. "Then send the next few through the system and release them. My data will support you. You should have guaranteed funding for the next five years. I'll talk to my friends on the Council and see to it."

Acres laughed and slid the cash envelope inside his jacket pocket. "Job security is a beautiful thing." He took a last drag on his cigarette and threw the butt onto the concrete alley behind the prison.

"Mind if I watch the next match?" Micah asked, waiting to be invited.

"Come on in. The fun is about to start."

Minutes later, Micah had an excellent view.

"Gentlemen, welcome to Hawkes Correctional Facility for Boys. My name is Sergeant Acres," he announced into a small desk top microphone. Two teenage boys waddled into a small, brightly lit room. The boys' feet were shackled to short chains that connected to a central chain wrapped around their waists. "Sit down and shut up!" Acres screamed.

The boys, between the ages of fifteen and seventeen, one black and one white, eyed each other, jockeying for the best orange, plastic chair. There were only two seats, with a table between them. Each tried to intimidate the other for the seat slightly closer to the door, but it was difficult to look bigger, tougher or smarter when walking was so restricted. The black boy, Malkin, was slightly thinner and quicker, and he lunged into the coveted seat, leaving Evan the remaining chair.

The smell of disinfectant filled the room. The halogen lights made everything look gray and surreal. Evan felt like a rat in the experimental lab of a mad man. He looked over at Malkin, whose wrists were bloody and bruised from his cuffs being too tight. He stared at him incredulously, but Malkin seemed to take little notice.

Sergeant Acres began to shout again over the speaker. "The city has little time and even less money to deal with the likes of you. Unfortunately, you have seen fit to arm yourselves and take to the streets. You thought it was a good idea to rob, steal, dominate and eventually kill your fellow citizens. That makes you criminals and criminals cost money."

At this, Malkin laughed.

Sergeant Acres watched them through a security camera and smirked, "You seem to think there are no consequences for taking another man's life. You—are—wrong. This city has a history of locking up young men like you who break the law, and then conveniently forgetting where it left the keys. Your 'rehabilitation' means we have to feed, clothe, and house you. The city can't afford to do so. It's already spent a lot of money feeding and educating you as school children. If it's forced to spend more money on you, then it wants to know that you're worth the investment. So now, gentlemen, answer this. How much does your life mean to you? The people you killed obviously meant nothing. What are you worth?

"According to your files, both of you attended DPS 45. You both took academy level classes. The city won't waste time on those who refuse to be educated. In this correctional facility, it will not pay for those who refuse to be rehabilitated. So, gentlemen, since you like power and planning out a hit, you qualify for the Hawkes Correctional Inmate Reduction Program."

The room next to them became illuminated. Evan could see that the two rooms were separated by a thick piece of glass. He could see the next, larger room filling with other boys dressed in the same orange scrubs. The incoming inmates were blinking and staring back at them.

Sergeant Acres continued his orientation speech, the speakers blaring in both rooms. "Each of you was hosed down when you arrived. If you're going to kill like animals then you'll be treated like animals. This is your one and only chance to prove the contrary. Men are worthy of another chance. Animals are disposable."

A third room on the other side of Malkin and Evan was suddenly bathed in light. There came a rushing sound from a nozzle in the ceiling as it moved slightly under the pressure. Two large dogs were inside fighting with one another. One dog was foaming at the mouth. The room full of teenagers began to yell and call out bets as to which dog would win. The rushing sound from the ceiling grew louder. Soon the two dogs were apart from each other and running to the corners of the room. They pawed at the door and tried to chew the bottom of its frame. One dog desperately ran to the glass next to Evan and Malkin and howled in fear, begging to be let out and clawing at the glass. The other threw himself hard against the window near the crowd of inmates. The boys cheered the dog on as he frantically tried to break through. In under a minute, the slightly smaller dog fell over. His paws scraping the glass as he slumped to the floor. The second dog immediately followed. Their bodies twitched and jerked as the gas suffocated them until they were dead.

Malkin watched the dogs cautiously. Evan sniffed the air deeply, trying to detect the smell of gas. His pulse quickened but he reassured himself it was merely a scare tactic.

Silence filled all three rooms. Sergeant Acres' voice came through the speaker with a gleeful lilt. "The soap with which you were hosed down during processing contained microbes. These microbes produce lactic acid when the human body is under stress." Evan ran his hand gingerly over his arms.

"If you're wondering what a microbe is, just think of it as a tiny bug that can be absorbed into your body and crawl under your skin."

Evan ran his fingers through his hair, checking to see if he noticed any crawling sensation.

"The true sign of a man is good performance and clear thinking while under pressure. A man will think his way through his problem. A dog will lose control, giving into his panic and strike out to save itself. Evan and Malkin, open your box and show your fellow inmates in the audience if you're a man or a dog."

Malkin opened the box and pulled out a vinyl scroll and a cardboard box. The scroll looked as if it came from recycled, cheap car seat upholstery. He wondered if the reduction program was sponsored in part by one of the local big car manufacturers. He unrolled it while Evan opened the coffee-stained box. When laid flat, the vinyl was a printed chess board complete with letter and numbers on the sides, turning it into a grid. The pieces in the box clunked together dully as the boys dug through and set up the chess board.

Chess was commonplace in Detroit. Some doctor somewhere had done a study back in the fifties convincing a booming city that it was the game of the educated and elite. Detroit was putting itself on the global map back then and the thought of its public schools teaching classes comparable to the likes of New York public schools was a defining moment. Fast forward sixty years, and the crumbling city was still using the tattered, recycled car floor mat boards in the hopes to teach strategy and logical thinking. Evan and Malkin had both used boards and pieces just like the ones before them since they'd entered public school in first grade. Since Evan opened the box, he set himself up with white pieces. White moved first. It was a slight advantage.

Malkin noticed but said nothing. "It all comes down to the endgame," he told himself.

Evan moved a pawn to the center of the board. He sadly recalled the hundreds of games he had played on the front porch with his grandpa. His father would sit in a chair in the corner, pretending to read his paper. He would look up and give advice to Evan between the middle and the end game when his grandfather had him cornered. His father had always told him, "Whoever has the center has the power." Evan wondered if he would ever have the chance to thank either of the men for those evenings together.

Malkin moved a pawn to open up a path for his knight. He waited to see if Evan would take note. School house chess demanded the classic control of the center of the board. Evan had been known in school for his high marks and chess trophies. Malkin, on the other hand, had scored lower in the eyes of his teachers. Malkin preferred street chess, where the strategies were planned only a couple moves deep and the death blow to the king appeared to come from nowhere. Street chess was fast and frantic; played from the emotional self where the cash rewards were pretty good if you knew how to hustle. Classic chess could take hours with strict logic at its core. Trophies and ratings were the rewards at school; useless trinkets for a kid trying to survive.

The thing about Malkin's 'shoot from the hip style' was if it worked, game over. Quick and lethal. Conversely, if the opponent saw it for what it was, then it meant starting a new plan all over again, putting oneself at a huge disadvantage.

A few moves between the two players and the inmates in the audience pulled their orange, plastic chairs up to the glass to get a closer look. Malkin set his bishop in place and leaned back in his chair. His heart began to race as Evan stared at the board. Malkin stared at Evan's face but Evan's eyes were hard to read. Evan reached for his rook. Malkin could feel a rush of adrenaline in anticipation of Evan's mistake and downfall. He wondered how the city killed off its incarcerated youth. He wondered but he really didn't care. People died every day. Why should he care so much about Evan? The goal was to survive and Malkin was about to win his life.

Evan stopped abruptly. He removed his glasses and rubbed the bridge of his nose in thought. His fingertips were a hair away from his rook but he didn't touch it. He knew the rules. If he touched a piece, he had to play it, even if he saw a better move at the last minute. Something felt wrong. Maybe it was the growing pounding in his head as he grappled with the realization that he was playing a death match. He looked at each of Malkin's pieces. He followed their paths. None looked suspicious. Then, he saw it. From way to the side, Evan saw Malkin's *fool's mate*. It was an old-time trick from the streets. Evan blocked the move and suddenly felt the pain in his head subside as he exhaled. Malkin, in contrast, jerked at the jab in his stomach. His kill had been thwarted.

The pain in his stomach felt as though a dull knife had been plunged into him, tearing away at his muscles. Evan looked on, in horror, as groups of microbes moved under the skin in Malkin's neck, racing to his torso. Malkin bared his teeth and clenched his fists. Evan tried to stand up and back away.

"Sit down!" the booming voice of Sergeant Acres shouted over the speaker.

The door to their room opened abruptly and two officers entered. Malkin and Evan's belly and ankle chains were shackled to the floor and padlocked.

Sergeant Acres' voice came over the speaker again, making everyone jump. "If you will look above your heads, gentlemen, you'll see that from the ceiling, two glass enclosures are suspended. With each piece taken by your opponent, the enclosure will descend. When the winner makes the final kill, the enclosure

...

above the loser will fall and completely seal. The nozzle at the top will release gas and kill the dog trapped in his cage. Proceed, gentlemen."

The boys in the audience stared up at the glass boxes and the protruding, one-eyed ventricle nozzles. Evan stared up and the throbbing returned in his head with a vengeance. He wondered how many microbes were swirling around, feasting on his gray matter. He assumed bugs needed to eat something. He shuddered and focused his attention at the chess board and counted the moves to his next strike. It was his turn and he pressed his lips together trying to think through the growing pounding in his brain.

Evan moved his knight toward the center with calm and focus. Malkin took it as a personal threat. Holding his stomach, he told himself that Evan would never be the man he was. He needed something that would scare Evan, something that would break that cool reserve.

Malkin brought out his queen, the most powerful piece on the board. As he placed her in the middle of his attack, he watched Evan's breathing begin to quicken. Beads of sweat formed on his forehead. He watched through dark, hooded eyes as Evan winced in pain under the stress. A conglomerate of microbes moved in unison, making Evan's scalp ripple. It made Malkin smile.

Evan tried breathing through the knife-like pain that seemed to be splitting his brain in two. He noticed that if he could control his racing heart, the pain was tolerable and he could think. His hands balled up in fists as he grappled for control. His mind wanted to shut down and hide. All he could feel was the searing, white pain. His opponent looked menacingly at him from across the table. Evan closed his eyes and began to breathe through his mouth to avoid vomiting. After a few minutes passed, the wave of pain decreased. Evan opened his eyes slowly for fear the bright light might set off his headache again. When there was no pain, he stared at the pieces on the board. After a few seconds, he regrouped and took Malkin's queen with a bishop.

A high-pitched whine sang sickly over Malkin's head as he watched the glass enclosure creep slowly towards him a few inches then stop. Malkin's chest heaved and he wanted to cry but he maintained his composure. A burst of pain ran down his arms as if his blood had turned to flame. He gripped the table, white knuckled. He had to relax, he told himself. He had to think of something else; something familiar.

He pretended he was staring down the barrel of a revolver. He imagined the cold steel leading up to the gun sight. He felt the solid weight of the handle. He thought of a target as he stared down the imaginary barrel of the gun. He made himself focus until he saw the face he was looking for. He aimed for Evan. The familiar survival exercise steadied his pulse and his body fell in line with his beating heart. Slowly, the pain eased and Malkin directed all of his energy towards defeating Evan.

Evan was staring at him.

Malkin showed cool calculation as he flexed his fingers and moved his arm robotically. Someone in the audience moved their chair closer to the glass and the boys in the audience laughed.

Malkin spun towards the boys and shouted, "What the hell are you looking at? It's my move, ain't it?"

Evan swallowed hard and stared down at the chess board quickly. He heard a few of the boys in the audience yell back. Malkin moved, this time capturing an unguarded knight of Evan's. The familiar whine sounded again from the ceiling as the gas chamber lowered. Evan pretended that the chamber above him didn't exist. One piece wasn't the end of the world. But he rubbed his temples as the microbes released their acid into the sockets behind his eyes. It made his eyes water. He took off his glasses and wiped the acid seeping from his tear ducts. He screamed.

More laughter and shouting erupted from the convicts in the audience. The inmates were beginning to take bets. Malkin felt his rage bubble to the surface. You bet on dog fights, he thought to himself. You bet on whether you could score a girl. You never bet on the fall of a brother, even the fall of Evan.

Evan switched his pieces around in a move called 'castling' to protect his king. Malkin moved his other knight and captured one of Evan's pawns. The enclosure above Evan squealed again. Malkin watched as his opponent stared at the death chamber dangle ever so closer to his head. Evan stared back at the board with swollen eyes, red and seeping with acid. His hands shook from the pain. He knew Malkin's move had not hurt his plan. It was a knee jerk reaction to losing his queen. But it was clear that given the opportunity, Malkin would show no mercy. Evan had to try to remember that. He needed to watch for the fast and furious street chess moves if he was going to make it out alive. He had to focus.

Sergeant Acres entered the room and set a black box with two silver buttons on the table next to the boys. "You have three minutes each to make your moves. If you fail to make your move in that time, the chamber will drop. If you fail to hit the button after you move and your time runs out, the chamber will drop. Do you have any questions?"

Neither Malkin nor Evan said anything. The two teens began breathing hard, each fighting back tears. The microbes in their bodies were riding on the tidal wave of blood, frantically surging through their veins as their hearts pounded under the added pressure.

Evan stared at the board as his chest heaved. Tears had turned to blood as the acid ate away at the tissue in his tear ducts. He couldn't think. He couldn't remember his plan. He glanced wildly at the clock as three minutes ticked away quickly. His hand shook as it hovered over the chess board. All he could think to do was play it safe. He moved a pawn one square and hit the button on the clock, nearly hyperventilating in the process.

Malkin rubbed his forehead and moved a pawn, hitting the clock. Evan took the pawn and stared at the board, looking hard for a way to end the game quickly. He ignored the chamber inching closer to Malkin. Evan formulated a way for several pieces to work together to capture Malkin's king. A noise from the glass outside broke his concentration. A boy was desperately banging the glass and pointing to the clock. Evan panicked, realizing he had forgotten to hit the button. Crippling pain rippled through his arm as he stretched his fingers and hit the button with only three seconds remaining. Malkin sat stoically, looking disappointed.

Malkin moved his king to protect it. Evan applied pressure by taking a rook. The chamber above Malkin lowered again and the boys outside laughed and exchanged bets. Evan tried not to notice as he visualized the moves in his head. As he stared, the pieces began to glow in his head, much like they had done when he was a boy in school. He had Malkin in three moves. Instead of giving him a huge sense of relief, he felt himself begin to weep. His survival on the streets had required him to kill for territory, for honor, for his gang. Jail was no different. The city required him to do the same; kill his enemy or be killed. The city's motives were far less noble. There was no glory, no new conquering of a street, no vendetta to settle. The city had found a way to reduce its inmate overcrowding problem; it made the bullets, and Evan was required to fire them, or take one in the heart himself.

Evan thought of forcing a stalemate. He could probably pull it off and if he did, maybe they could both be set free. He looked at the clock and at Malkin. He looked at the pool of blood at the edge of the board from his weeping eyes. Malkin stared at the blood too with a smirk. The smirk made Evan reconsider any merciful end game. The city wanted one winner and one loser. He considered letting Malkin win for a moment. His hand hovered over the pieces as he deliberated. The nightmares he had suffered from the shooting in the street had been the driving force to turning himself in. Could he kill again? He glanced at the clock ticking away. If he won, what was the prize? Jail time? Maybe death was a better option.

He stared into Malkin's hungry face. Malkin stared desperately at the board. It was clear to Evan that Malkin was lost. Malkin had no big plan and there was nothing he could do about it besides play it out to the end.

Evan took a deep breath, made up his mind and made his move. Knowing he would win, there was no pain anywhere in his body as he hit the button on the clock. Malkin stared at the chess board and a wave of realization flooded his face. He looked up at Evan.

Malkin stared at him with a mixed expression of envy, pride and anger. Sweat pouring down his cheeks, he stared out at the faces in the crowd. Some were pounding on the glass as they pointed to the board. A small boy in front urgently pointed to the time running out on the clock.

Malkin moved his rook near the center of the board without any benefit to himself. He hit the clock. More microbes visibly clustered down his neck and into his chest. He threw his head back and choked, pounding his fist on the table. As he coughed, blood covered his lips and ran down his chin. Evan zeroed in and took the only piece protecting Malkin's king. He hit the clock with tears running down his cheeks. The chamber dropped down closer to Malkin's head.

Malkin gripped the corners of the table to steady himself. He stared up into the death chamber above him. The thick glass sat like a crown dangling just above his head. For a moment, the teen straightened his back and looked older and taller than his age. He set his jaw as he turned and stared into the video camera. He placed his index finger on his king, then knocked it over, declaring defeat. He closed his eyes and the death chamber fell, sealing him inside like a tomb. The nozzle at the top of the chamber shook and a smoky gas swirled around Malkin.

Evan screamed that his opponent was no 'dog'! He shouted to Sergeant Acres that they were being treated like animals! He writhed in fury and agony, but his protests were petty as he was confined to his chair. Without hope, he merely screamed over and over again for help! He watched Malkin choke.

Blood from Malkin's lungs splattered the gas chamber and slowly ran down the glass.

Evan sobbed and reached his hand out to his dying opponent.

Malkin didn't fight. He didn't cry. He merely closed his eyes as he coughed and gasped, never once losing his dignity or his vengeful pride. If he couldn't choose how he would die, then he would choose when. It was a final act of spite against a soulless city.

Evan and the rest of the boys watched as they dragged Malkin's body away. The officer dragged him away by one foot. Acres entered the room by way of the first door and unlocked Evan's chain to the floor. The boy was escorted to a dark, metal room where five other boys nervously sat.

Micah peered in at them.

No beds, and a hole in the floor as a bathroom; he made note of it all while he watched them. A disgusting smell hit his senses and he stepped back.

"Dinner!" Acres announced.

The boys looked up but didn't move towards the trays set out on the floor. They had just watched their fellow inmate being gassed without a second thought by their keepers.

When Micah had seen enough, he nodded to Acres and found his way to the alley.

He dialed his phone. "The foot soldiers arrive tomorrow night. Have the others arrived?"

"Yes," Kevin replied.

"Good. I'll pick you up in thirty minutes. *The game* will be spread over several days and the team will need a place to return to and rest. I doubt you or your neighbors want vampiric guards surrounding your house once *the game* begins."

"I don't really care about any of that anymore," Kevin said. "We do need to have a talk, though. There's something you need to see."

Chapter 13

Ruth watched the night vision video feed as Helen and Ray both slept in their separate pens. Each small cage was suspended above the floor. Each swayed ever so slightly as the human captives breathed deeply in their REM sleep. She smirked at the captain. "Do you know why Kobe beef is so special?"

"Who cares?" he said honestly.

"Don't be a tool. Take an interest," Ruth scolded.

The captain looked at her with mocked concentration.

"Aside from being bred in a very unique region with environmental purity, the cows are fed a diet of beer and massaged with *sake*," she explained. "They're free-roaming until a few weeks before they're to be slaughtered, where they're then penned and confined. The beer thickens the blood and brings oxygen to the muscles. The massage and confinement helps the meat to marble while the sake acts like a tenderizer."

The captain gave a half smile of gratitude for his enlightenment.

Ruth continued. "Considering my plans for our two guests, I feel as though they should be as tasty and tempting as possible." She paused and then said, "Put them in their rooms before the drugs wear off."

"Royal treatment even for the livestock, all in the name of the game of kings," the captain mused.

Ruth nodded. Maybe the captain wasn't as blunt as he seemed.

Ray was dreaming. He was snorkeling back home in the ocean. The water was warm and familiar. He swam through a school of brightly-colored fish. He could feel their tails flicking against his forearms and through his hair. The sensation was exhilarating. He turned to look at them, and was contemplating another pass through the school, when he noticed they weren't fish at all. He reached out and grabbed one as it swam by. It was a money bundle. There were hundreds of them with rubber bands at their middle. He laughed as elation took over. He was literally swimming in money.

As the rays of glorious sunshine sliced through the azure blue water, a shadow loomed overhead. The shadow of a figure came into view and turned towards him. Ray wasn't worried. He had plenty of money. He would hand the diver a couple of fistfuls. After all, he was generous.

As the diver approached, Ray could see it was a woman, a beautiful woman. If this was heaven, he should have died sooner, he thought. But as the diver moved closer, he saw that it was actually a mermaid. She swam to him, her hair billowing and buoyant like swirls of grenadine in vodka. She smiled at him, reached out for him. Ray swam towards her in spite of himself. She was beckoning him away from the swimming bundles.

He could swim just a little farther to reach her. The money wouldn't be too far, he figured. Their hands touched and she pulled him towards her effortlessly. He kissed her and she returned the kiss. He took in her beauty like a work of art. Reaching out to touch her again, his fingertips caressed her exposed breasts. To his disappointment, her expression changed. The mermaid cocked her head to one side, her face contorted, her pupils dilated, and her teeth elongated.

She ripped away his breathing mask. Ray screamed and gulped in a large amount of sea water. He jerked his hand away from her as the last of his air bubbles escaped from his garbled scream. He swam hard, up towards the surface. But the swimming, flitting bundles of money wouldn't let him reach the surface. He was drowning. The mermaid grasped his foot and dragged him deeper into the depths. As his lungs began to fill with water, he felt her jagged teeth sink into his neck and tear away the flesh.

Being eaten alive and no one to hear him scream, Ray woke from his watery grave of a dream with jolt. His ocean was exchanged for lying in a lavish, albeit sweat-soaked, bed. Beside him was Helen.

She stared at him. From her wild-eyed expression, she too had been dreaming of something both wonderful and simultaneously terrible. The two lovers said nothing to one another for a long time, both wondering truly about reality. Both the water and the bed felt equally real for Ray. They were shaken from their silence by a knock at the door.

"Room service," a polite voice said.

Helen and Ray looked to one another questioningly. Helen pulled back the covers to find herself dressed in a silk robe. At her bedside was a pair of matching slippers. She had never seen either before. Wearing a strangers robe and slippers, she answered the door. A young man pushed a cart into the room with silver dome-covered plates and glass pitchers of water and juice.

"A message for you," the man said. He handed Helen an envelope, then smiled at them both and promptly left the room.

"I would have tipped him had I known where my pants were," Ray tried to joke. "Do you have any idea what the hell is going on?"

Helen shook her head. She opened the envelope to find that she and Ray were scheduled for a complimentary day at the spa.

Neither could form the words to describe their dreams of bright lights and drinking a strange-tasting liquid, of confined spaces and complete darkness. It dawned on them collectively that they were starving. Without an exchange of any further conversation, they uncovered their breakfasts and ate ravenously.

Kevin held up a finger as if to tell Micah to be quiet and listen.

"Here it is," Riley said. "I wanted to read this at Dad's memorial but Mom said it would be too hard on me. She said children don't read things at their father's funerals. Here, you read it." Riley slid the book across the patio table as Robby sat back in his chair while sipping a beer.

Rose cleared her throat and read,

There is a place where the sidewalk ends.
And before the street begins,
And there the grass grows soft and white,
And there the sun burns crimson bright,
And there the moon-bird rests from his flight,
To cool in the peppermint wind.
Let us leave this place where the smoke blows black,
And the dark street winds and bends.
Past the pits where the asphalt flowers grow,
We shall walk with a walk that is measured and slow,
And watch where the chalk-white arrows go,
To the place where the sidewalk ends.
Yes we'll walk with a walk that is measured and slow,
And we'll go where the chalk-white arrows go,
For the children, they mark, and the children, they know,

The place where the sidewalk ends.

— Shel Silverstein —

Rose could feel a lump in her throat but she smiled at Riley anyway. "Your dad would have loved that."

"I know you're worried about me playing *the game,* but I'm not a kid anymore. My dad is gone and it feels like he took part of me with him." Riley started to cry for the first time since she'd heard the news that her father had died. "I need to know that you guys trust me. I'm a good chess player. I can beat him!" Tears were streaming down her face but her gaze pierced Robby and Rose. "I won't let anything happen to you. I promise."

Robby shook his head and leaned in close across the table. "Hang on there, young lady. You can't make that promise. Whatever happens, you just do your best. That's all any of us can do."

Rose tried to add to the sentiment but her tears turned into a coughing fit.

Robby gripped her hand in support. "Rose agrees with me."

Rose nodded.

Kevin walked back into the house, motioning for Micah to follow. "Do you see?" Kevin whispered, irate. "There's no way she has business playing in that match. The burden is too great for a kid, let alone one grieving over her father."

Riley stepped into the kitchen to get her leftover ice cream and stopped. She dropped back when she heard the two men say her name. She listened intently.

"I didn't get that at all from what she said," Micah argued. "On the contrary, I think she needs this game to happen and she needs the chance to get even."

"She's risking her life!" Kevin raged. "She doesn't even know what life is at her age."

"She knows she's facing it without a father."

"Yes, but she still has her mother. A mother, I might add, who needs her right now. Do you expect the poor woman to bury her ex-husband and her daughter in the same month?"

"I expect you to have a little faith in a brilliant kid. You're a teacher after all," Micah said.

Riley returned to the garden.

"What's this? No ice cream?" Robby asked. "Don't tell me you're watching your girlish figure," he teased.

"Someone must have eaten it," she lied. "It's cool. I'm going to go study anyways. Good night."

"Let's hope she bloody well does study those past games of her father," Robby said, sounding a bit doubtful for the first time.

Rose, tired from coughing and from the long day, put her head on his shoulder.

He absentmindedly kissed her forehead.

Kevin sat alone in Delta's reading chair, drinking a short, neat glass of bourbon. He looked at Delta's picture and spoke to it as if his dead wife could hear him. "What have I gotten myself into? I'll have blood on my hands for the rest of my life. I can't stop that now. But how much blood? I could take Riley tonight. I could take her to her mother and send them some place far away. And then I...I could...I could end this. I could find a way home to you." He heard himself and had to admit he sounded desperate and unstable. He took a large sip from his glass.

A light evening wind blew through the sheer, lace curtains. A dull thud made Kevin jump, tearing him away from his self-destructive thoughts. He looked down to find that a book had fallen off a shelf and had landed at his feet. Shockingly, the book opened by itself and several pages turned to a specific passage. With shaking hands, Kevin read the page he was given.

"So did I really die? I just barely made it in this particular universe, but did I die in another equally real universe where this book was never written?" Kevin continued on to the next page. "If I'm in these two different places in two parallel universes, then one version of me will survive. If you apply the same argument to all other ways I can die in the future, it seems there will always be at least one parallel universe where I never die. Since my consciousness exists only where I'm alive, does that mean that I'll subjectively feel immortal?" Kevin looked to the cover, *Our Mathematical Universe* by Max Tegmark.

Delta certainly had read this book and many like it to understand Kevin's world. Now, she was preaching to the master. Kevin was humbled by her elegant understanding of a passion he had never thought her worthy of sharing with him.

"Riley may become immortal but how am I to know if it's this reality, my reality. What if I'm the reason she dies? More blood on my hands, Delta."

Another book fell to the floor, this time across the room. Kevin stood up from the chair and held the book open to the first page as Delta, her spirit riding on the evening breeze, flipped the pages. A book of collaborative works by photographers of Detroit flipped its own pages until it settled on one particular image. In black and white, several pre-teens, about Riley's age, joined a few women, all of them wearing 1950's hairstyles and sitting on cars in their hooped skirts. Two girls held a sign. It read, "Nothing Stops the Motor City." Strikingly, the girl on the left could have passed for Riley.

Delta had made her point in her quiet yet convincing way. If it was Riley's destiny to become immortal, then Kevin owed it to her to play his part. The laws of theoretical mathematics and physics would see to the rest of her fate. If he refused to help, she would likely play *the game* without him. She was determined, and in that message Kevin understood. It was better to protect and support Riley than to leave her to her own devices; alone like her father had been alone.

Kevin closed the book and looked out the window into the night. His reflection stared back at him. For a moment, he could see Delta in his eyes, and he suddenly missed her more than the day she had died.

"I would have given anything for this to be your reality, your parallel universe, where you became immortal," he said, unable to hold back the tears. He looked at Delta's picture once more, and her eyes told him that she loved him. She was here, and in her own way, she had always been with him. That would have to be enough, Kevin reminded himself. That would have to be enough.

Chapter 14

Geraldine lay on the floor shivering in pain from cold and hunger. Her eyes burned. It was difficult to see. Imaginary bugs were driving their tiny needle-like stingers into her scalp. The ringing in her ears had just started, adding another layer of misery. She pulled the blanket off the bed and wrapped it around her thin body tightly. Maybe she could hold herself together in every sense of the word, if she could just make it tight enough.

Through the ringing siren of her mind, she listened intently for James. He had left hours ago. The pricking of thirst had gone from slight to a raging fire in his absence. What if he didn't come back before sunrise? What if he stayed away, letting her whither in her undead anguish? She would have cried if she had possessed the ability. The dealer had become the addict and she fell into a deep pit of self-loathing.

She considered ignoring his order to stay in their room. She would just go out and make a quick kill. She could be careful. She was sure she could. But James had warned her. The members of the team had told her their stories of getting caught. She would spend more than one night feeling this way if she did get caught. Her throat smoldered, raw and agonizing. James' treatment of her was deplorable. She decided that she would take her survival into her own hands.

Throwing the blanket off herself, she smoothed out her t-shirt and jeans. She took a deep breath and opened the window. Gauging the distance between her second floor window and the ground, she pressed her long nails into the window frame. She crouched down as if to spring when her world turned upside down. She landed hard on her back. Before she registered what was happening, she was flying backwards again, this time landing hard against the wall. James had returned, livid.

He grabbed her face, checking for traces of blood from a recent feeding. His hands were strong and she could smell the blood he had just consumed through his skin.

"I didn't! I didn't leave," she whimpered. "I was starving and you left me here to rot!"

"I left you here so I can feed enough to keep us both alive, you naive bitch!" Rolling up his sleeve, Geraldine closed her eyes and braced for another blow. Instead, the scent of blood overwhelmed her senses. James offered his inner arm to his convert and she didn't need to be asked twice. She drank deeply, gripping his wrist. Blood ran down her chin. When James felt himself slightly weaken, he pulled away, holding up his other hand in a warning not to challenge him.

Still slightly hungry, Geraldine licked the sticky remains around her mouth. She sucked the blood-soaked collar of her shirt as she tried to calm her bloodlust.

There was little reprieve from the anger that consumed James. "We're only two days away from *the game* and you have no control let alone a connection to Cadel. This is the last feeding I'll give to you. Find a way into his head by way of his heart or his bed, but do it. If you fail to meet the terms of our contract, I'll lock you in the *facility* myself."

"You can't still think that Cadel is the real power here?" Geraldine desperately pleaded. "Ruth has set up the entire *game*. Rumors say she has gathered an A-list of global power players, celebrities and society members the likes that have never been put together in history."

"When the actual *game* is being played, who will be the hero? The person who invited the people is the one who just brought home a death match championship. Ruth may have set *the game* in motion but we need the vampire team to lose."

"Lose? Are you crazy?" Geraldine stared at James.

"I want Ruth to take a historic downfall, and I need Cadel to make it happen. So tell me, would you rather the man calling the moves on the board feel the need to protect or kill you?"

Geraldine had no idea what was motivating James, but was sure that if she wasn't his ally he would surely find another queen. Maybe Cadel would let her feed if she could seduce him. Stripping off her clothes, she scavenged through her suitcase and found her best lingerie. She sat on the bed, pulling on a garter and black stockings, thong bikini panties and a black-lace bra. She pulled her hair down and let it sit messy over her shoulders and breasts. "Will this do?" she asked James through hooded eyes.

"Get him under our thumb tonight or I'll crown a new queen by tomorrow night," James replied harshly.

As Geraldine made her way out of the royal bedroom, she plotted for her survival. Choosing immortality was a mistake. She might have lived longer in her human form than the one accompanying her shadow down the hall. Regret wouldn't keep her alive.

She found Cadel's door with two guards at the threshold. Waltzing up to the first guard boldly, she asked him if there was a password. He said nothing, too stunned to see the queen in such little attire. The other guard was similarly affected. She smiled. "The game master and I have a few moves we have to discuss." Neither of them stopped her as she walked in and closed the door. She knew they wouldn't.

Unlike James, who was a younger, modern vampire, Cadel was traditional. He was lounging, reading the paper Maria had left for him while still in his coffin. When he looked up, he couldn't conceal his surprise. Uncomfortably, he glanced over at the computer monitor. The screen was broken up into several small squares, each showing Maria sleeping from different angles and also the security detail.

"It must be very difficult for you," Geraldine sighed, tracing a manicured nail tip along the screen while pulling out a small desk chair and sitting down in front of it. "I mean, James will occasionally fuck me, but really, he loves someone who is already dead. But you…" She paused to play with the end of her hair. "You love a woman whom you can't fuck for fear of killing her in the act. If you turn her, she'll just go off to be with another. She won't need you anymore. And so day after day I watch you as you pine for her. It seems as though your body must…" She stopped.

"Must what?" Cadel asked, trying to hold his composure.

Geraldine leaned forward slightly, giving him a glimpse at her perky breasts. She let go of the end of her hair and let it cascade across her chest as she replied, "Your body must ache."

"You're a woman and so you see the nature that is a man, whether he be human or vampire," Cadel admitted.

With graceful speed, Geraldine stood and leaned on the desk as if she were looking at the sleeping Maria. Her high heels and thong bikini revealed her long legs and the small of her back.

"Do you ever long for a release?" she asked, not turning around to look him in the eye for a few long seconds. Then she turned slowly to address him further. "When I was alive, I found that to be alive is to throw away the stresses of the days and nights." She took off her left shoe. "Some of my clients paid me quite well to keep them in drugs that would give them the illusion of release. But that was just a chemical reaction." She took off her right shoe. "To be French is to know the secret to real pleasure and from the height of pleasure comes the serenity of release. Wouldn't you agree?" She unhooked her bra and tossed it to the floor.

Cadel was gripping the side of his coffin. He tried to find Maria in one of the many security screens but Geraldine was now sitting on the table before the monitor.

She opened her legs. "Couldn't we help each other? Let me give you the pleasure your human love can not. And in exchange, you can fill up the emptiness in my heart, for my love cries for another." She was sure to say the last bit with a thicker French accent, as if her sincerity might be more convincing. She climbed into Cadel's coffin and crawled onto him on all fours. "Please?" she whispered.

As she leaned into kiss him, he gripped her throat tightly. There was deliberation in his hold of her.

"A kiss is for love and that is something reserved for her, not you," he said.

"Surely there are things you would like to do with her besides kiss her," Geraldine pursued.

Cadel closed his eyes and his grip was no longer at her throat but gripping her body. The lingerie was torn away effortlessly as he ravaged her. She became disoriented as she felt her body become weightless. She hadn't grown accustomed to flying but Cadel carried them both to the ceiling effortlessly. He pressed her back against the ceiling and drove himself deep inside of her. Once their two bodies had become one, he dug his talons into the plaster ceiling and made love to her wildly. The gravity pulled on her as he countered and thrust himself into her from beneath. It was both terrifying and orgasmic. With each thrust she felt as if she might fall and yet the lack of a bed made the sensation all the more appealing.

She took him again, after they had rested; this time in his coffin. From the corner of her eye, she could see movement in the monitor. Geraldine was slow. She was calculating. She built up his pleasure over time, until like her clients in Paris, he craved her and what she offered above anything else in the world. Just as Cadel reached a climax, Geraldine smiled and joined him. She heard the clicking of the tumblers in the lock, and like the coming dawn, her plan to control Cadel was as welcoming as the sun.

Upstairs, James heard a scream, followed by the sound of running. Unsure what Geraldine had decided to do, he chanced the charring of his skin in the rising sun and ran downstairs. He found Maria, hysterical and scrambling for her keys in her purse. Clearly Geraldine had successfully seduced Cadel. James found Maria's keys and cell phone for her, then he programmed his number in quickly and gave both to the frantic girl. With tears streaming down her face, she stumbled to her car and drove out of sight, gravel flying behind the vehicle as she did so.

Some time later, Geraldine, wrapped in Cadel's robe and wearing sunglasses, sauntered into James' kitchen. "Well done," he said. "How will you keep him from blaming you?"

"He's a smart man. He knows he only has himself to blame," she replied. "Let him lie awake in his coffin all day. Tonight, I'll twist what is already broken."

"Now that sounds like a queen talking," he smiled.

"The prodigal son returns," Ruth mused scathingly as Micah showed his security badge and passed the guards in the stadium.

"You told me to take care of things and I did. Now I'm back and I have things to report," Micah replied, calmly.

"Things to report to me? Or things to report to the Council?" Ruth tested.

"I wouldn't have tracked you down before the tour if I wasn't reporting to you and you alone."

"How can I be sure?"

"Because I have exclusive information as well as this." Micah placed a small box in her hand. "Open it."

Reluctantly, Ruth did so and held up a pendant on a gold chain. "What's this? A dove of peace?" she asked sarcastically.

Micah paused and breathed deeply. "No. It was Emily's. It was given to her by the Royal Music Conservatory. I thought to bury it with her, but instead I thought it might look better on you. A gesture from the heart, if only mine were still beating." He smirked meekly, hoping that the gift was convincing.

"What about the information?" Ruth asked, her expression blank.

"Robby contacted me. I know security has been searching for the human team base. Here is the address to the house where they'll remain until *the game* is finished."

Ruth said nothing and Micah watched her nervously. She dialed her cell phone and dispersed the security detail to Kevin's house. A few minutes later, the captain confirmed the address of the human captain, Robby. She hung up.

When Jeremiah arrived, he looked surprised to find Micah and Ruth at the stadium before him. "Shall we convene the Council tour?" he asked cautiously.

Ruth clipped the necklace around her neck and gave a quick glance at Micah. "I second the motion."

"I'm concerned about news coverage," Micah said. "The inner city death toll is rising. Can we take our vampiric guests to the outer cities to feed?"

Jeremiah was enraged. "This is the very reason we have to have this *game*! Have the spectators no respect or discretion?"

"They will when I'm done with them," Ruth confirmed, making both counterparts stop and stare.

"Then the human team is assembled?" Jeremiah asked.

"Yes. I just received confirmation today. The security detail has arrived, too. When will their gear be delivered?" Micah asked.

Ruth smiled. "Tell them their uniforms and weaponry will arrive tomorrow. Oh, and Micah, can you pay them a personal call? Make sure they know which part of their weapons are the dangerous, pointy sides. After all, we don't want them self-mutilating themselves before *the game* even begins."

Maria's phone vibrated like it had a hundred times. She refused to talk to Cadel. Glancing down from the road, she noticed the number was different. In spite of her best intuition, she answered it.

"Maria, just listen to me," James said. "Cadel is beside himself and admits to being in love with you. This is your one chance to make him grovel for that love as well as get revenge on the queen. Are you interested?"

"Why should I believe you?" Maria spat.

"Next to you, I'm the only other person who wants to see the queen and the entire *game* fail. Come back to Detroit. Come to *the game.* Help me and I guarantee you and your love will be on a plane back to Italy this time next week. The choice is yours."

"Why would you want to kill your own queen?" Maria asked.

James hesitated before replying. His voice cracked slightly. "She gave me the heroin junky in the alley; she was the one who recorded the kill. The bar security camera had been broken for months. Geraldine turned me in and in the process killed the only true love I will ever know."

Chapter 15

Robby absentmindedly applied pressure to the small of Rose's back as he stood next to her. He could feel her shudder. The Council had called in the royals for their photo shoot. Being a model had never been a dream of Rose's. Even if she had envisioned such a job, it wouldn't have taken place in what had once been the grinding room of a meat packing house. Cold, sterile and death still lingered in the air made her wonder if the vampires had chosen the room for effect.

Geraldine, James, Rose and Robby were posed and set in place. They were wearing their opposing uniforms and staring into the bright lights and cameras. Members of the Council watched from the edges of the room.

"I thought vampires didn't show up in photographs," Robby remarked, trying to find some humor in an otherwise uncomfortable situation.

"That's one of the many myths," Jeremiah replied from somewhere beyond the blinding lights.

Geraldine sneered. "What's not a myth is that half of the spectators looking at this program will see your pictures and think it more a menu than a show."

Ruth cleared her throat in disapproval of the queen and the conversation ended abruptly.

When the photo shoot was over, the four were lead to the room that had formerly been used for hanging meat to age. Hooks of various sizes hung from chains cascading from the ceiling. Ruth gave the human team a hungry look of intimidation. Geraldine and Ruth exchanged glances as if in telepathic conversation. It didn't go unnoticed by Jeremiah as he handed the couples their team packets.

"These are the rules of *the game*. As the royal couple, you'll en-sure that your team understands them before stepping foot onto the field. Understood?" All four nodded. "Good, let's review the basics. The vampiric team will be wearing helio-bond-infused uniforms. The solar energy cables have been reduced to thread-size and woven into the very fibers. Additional bonds are at your neck and feet. They'll be activated as you leave your team room."

"What sort of restrictions will the humans have to keep them in line?" Geraldine asked defensively.

Robby burst out laughing, catching everyone off guard. "How about half the fucking stadium wants to eat us? Think that might keep us from running away?" His laughter grew louder and he slapped his knee. "It's a whole new meaning to the phrase *fast food*, eh, mate?"

Rose stared at him incredulously but James laughed in spite of himself.

Ruth interrupted. "You're making quite a mockery of *the game*!" she scolded. She turned to Geraldine with mock compas-sion in her voice. "Rest assured, any of our team members remain-ing after the first part of *the game* will return to their base to find a meal ready for them."

Rose made a small gasp. "By meal, you mean some poor, inno-cent bystander."

Ruth was losing her temper. "A meal you apparently very much hope to enjoy if your game master could pull off a win, let me remind you!" Ruth was seething.

Jeremiah stepped between the two and asked, "It's come to my attention that your game master hasn't registered with your team. Have you a game master or shall we consider this your forfeit?" The room fell silent and Rose took a deep, cleansing breath.

"We certainly do have a game master. She has her contract with her," Robby smiled.

"Good!" Jeremiah beamed. "Cadel, could you please come forward for your confirmation as well?"

James watched as Cadel appeared from out of the shadows. He was wearing a pinstripe suit for the occasion. As he passed James and Geraldine, his gaze rested on the vampiric queen for a few long seconds. Her eyes smoldered in response to which he turned away quickly. As Cadel took an oath before the Council and the royals, James quickly sent a text to Maria. Speak to his heart, and soon, or you may never speak to him again. Timing is crucial.

After Cadel made his promise to play to the highest standards of the FIDE rules of chess, Robby called for the human game master. James looked on as Cadel reached in his pocket and looked at his phone. He hoped it was Maria. Cadel's mind was telepathically impenetrable. James would have to just hope she had sent him a message.

The door from another corridor opened and Riley walked in meekly. Shadows of swinging meat hooks played across her face and body as she straightened her back and stood beside Robby. Micah confirmed that she was their choice. Cadel and Ruth both laughed.

Cadel was obviously offended. "You can't possibly be serious. I'll look like a fool!"

Riley handed her contract to Jeremiah. "One looks like a fool, only if they lose, and my father taught me never to lose."

Her determination stopped Ruth from laughing. She walked over to Riley and tucked a strand of the girl's hair behind her ear. "Did your father also teach you that it's rude to talk to adults like that? When you do lose, I'll truly enjoy killing you myself."

Robby pulled Riley away from Ruth, his immense hands steering her small frame by the shoulders. When she was safely behind him, he stepped closer to Ruth. "I wonder if in all the world a human man has ever killed a vampire with his bare hands. I promise you, if you ever talk to that girl like that ever again, we'll definitely find out."

"Spoken like a true idiot," Ruth rebuffed. "You would have to use your hands because you certainly don't have the brains to outsmart me. Do you know it was your adulterous wife and her lover, *your* manager, I might add, who helped me to track your every move? She was there all along, right under your nose." She waited a few seconds for the news to sink in. "Love stinks, doesn't it? On the bright side, you might really enjoy the opening ceremonies."

For fear a match to the death might break out before *the game* even started, Jeremiah concluded the meeting and began escorting Robby, Rose and Riley out to meet with their team. When they had disappeared around the corner, Ruth turned to James and said, "No matter what happens at the end of *the game*, bring me that girl. She's a small meal, but one I deserve to feast upon. Who knows what she'd be capable of if we let her live to adulthood."

"She looks small enough. Fetch her yourself. I'm a king, not a dog," James retaliated.

Ruth clicked her remote and the full strength of the heliobonds, woven into James' uniform, ignited, sending him to his knees. Ruth walked slowly around him as Geraldine watched, terrified. "You are whatever I say you are. Your life is still my possession. Bring her to me or plan on the rest of your eternity being spent inside a *facility*, I personally oversee." She glanced at Geraldine and smiled. "For good measure, I'll be sure to have Cadel torture you in *the game*, just to help jog your memory."

Geraldine watched as James began to shake, losing his composure. Whether it was from pain or rage, she wasn't sure. As Ruth sauntered to the door, a click could be heard in the room and James collapsed, spread eagle, onto the floor. Gasping and shaking, he rolled onto his back slowly.

"Do you still think the chess master has all the power?" Geraldine asked. "From where I'm standing, I'd say the best odds are with her. That's where my money's at."

James pulled himself up and stood, thankful that his recovery was quicker thanks to the feeding he had indulged in the night before. "I'm very aware who you've sided with and what you've done. I know it was you who turned me in to save your own skin. Fear not, my darling, you're on my list."

Geraldine laughed skeptically. "If you wanted to kill me, you'd have done it when I was human."

"No!" James yelled, losing his temper as the memory of Quinn and his sentencing flooded his mind. "I want you to suffer. I want you to know what it feels like to have it all and to be careless with it. I want you to realize how precious immortality is. Imagine having the chance to love someone forever, you and your love never having to worry about growing old or getting sick. I threw away my chance because of you. Enjoy your immortality. Cling to it, and when you begin to fall in love with forever, I'll be there to take it away from you, just like you took it away from me!"

Hired security checked IDs and guest lists on the human side of the stadium as the sun began to set. Micah watched from the surveillance cameras. He and Jeremiah had invited the human patrons to arrive earlier, in the hopes to avoid conflict between them and the vampire audience. Jeremiah entered Micah's mind; he confirmed all was well and then made his mind blank. When Micah felt Jeremiah leave him and his thoughts, Jeremiah texted Kevin to check on the team. They had to be getting nervous.

As the crowd assembled, Evan peeked through the double doors from the ready room. Senators, dignitaries he had only seen on television, rock stars, actors and a plethora of people dressed in designer attire took their seats behind the sealed glass enclosures.

Amongst the human elite, was Maria. She had arrived early and had taken a seat in the center, nearly exactly across from where Cadel would sit in his small room with a large window to play the chess match. She strained, trying to see if she could spot him in the room yet. From across the large field it was too difficult to tell. She opened her phone and texted Cadel. Enter my mind, she typed and hit send.

Where are you? he replied.

Reach out to me and you'll see.

A warm sensation washed over Maria. It had, in the past, been the happiest feeling in the world. She loved Cadel so deeply that she opened her mind to him freely. This time, though, she was guarded. She held her thoughts close, only revealing to him what she wanted him to see...her love for him. He responded by showing her a scene of her in a tight embrace, under the large, harvest moon.

His voice accompanied the vision. "Look how beautiful you'll be when I've turned you; perfection preserved and frozen for all eternity."

Maria manipulated the vision. She showed Geraldine standing near a tree, just behind them, her silhouette made out by the moonlight.

Maria struggled not to let her anger and feelings of betrayal break her concentration. "We'll never have our forever until *she* is dead. If you kill her in *the game*, then I'll know that you love me. If she lives at the end of the match, you'll never see me again." Then she closed her mind completely. Cadel called out to her, but she didn't reply. After a long while, Maria's phone vibrated. She read the text. What you're asking me to do is suicide.

Maria typed back, What I'm asking you to do is choose. Her or me.

Cadel stared at the chess pieces aligned on his board. The large digital camera was already on and casting a holographic image above the field just outside his window. He took out his notes and began to rearrange his opening. He thought of Riley. Would a father teach a child the ancient games or the modern ones? Would he be gentle to his daughter and let her win? Cadel had never fathered children before he was turned. His opponent was as foreign to him as an alien. Chess was more than placing pieces strategically on a board. It was playing the person across the board as well. How easily could he frighten her? How many moves could a child see in the future? How much could he risk looking like he was playing for his team, only to kill off his most valuable piece and risk losing everything?

Rose took a handful of pills and a glass of water in preparation for the long night ahead. Robby listened to the crowds gather, their footsteps sounding like thunder. If this was rugby he would have suggested a *Haka*, but his team of unlikely heroes wouldn't have the first clue about the ritual dance he'd done with his *All Blacks'* mates. He looked up as Evan moved quickly out of the doorway.

Rose looked concerned. "Riley, honey, what are you doing here?"

Robby and Rose looked to Kevin for an explanation as, he too, slipped into the room.

Riley smiled, touching the sleeve of Rose's white uniform. She didn't give an explanation, she only sat in the middle of the floor with a book. Most of the boys from the Hawkes Correctional Facility rolled their eyes and tied and re-tied their shoelaces nervously. Some of the others paced. No one said anything, but their expressions were desperate and full of doubt.

Riley opened her book and began to read aloud. "It's a great huge game of chess that's being played—all over the world—if this is the world at all, you know. Oh, what fun it is! How I wish I was one of them! I wouldn't mind being a *pawn*." The boys from the prison looked up, hearing their position referred to. "If only I might join—though of course I should like to be a *queen* the most."

Rose smiled, albeit skeptically.

Riley continued reading. "She glanced rather shyly at the real queen as she said this, but her companion only smiled pleasantly, and said, 'That's easily managed. You can be the White Queen's pawn, if you like, as Lily is too young to play; and you're in the Second Square to begin with: when you get to the Eighth Square, you'll be a Queen— (Looking Glass 2.61-62)' "

When Riley finished, no one said anything. She shot up like a rocket, her feet coming off the floor as she did so. "Don't you get it?" she shouted.

Evan laughed. "I think we might be past bed time stories little master."

"Then you're nothing but a stupid boy," Riley spat, showing her age. "What Alice is saying is that we're *all* just a bunch of pawns. A pawn, the lowest piece on the board is the *only* piece that, if it makes it to the eighth row, the king's row, it becomes the most powerful piece on the board."

"So you can have more than one queen on the board?" Kevin asked.

"Yes. And there are lots of ways weak pieces become strong when they work together," Riley continued. "I just wanted you to know that I plan to win and take all of you with me." She ran to Robby and hugged him. "The queen protects her king at all costs." She held his hand and pulled him to Rose. "And the king stays alive in the hopes of one more day with his queen." She pulled the bishops and knights off of their bench and had them join Robby and Rose. "The bishops distract the eye of the people while the knights swoop in and attack from sides." The rest of the team, the pawns and rooks, followed the example and joined in. Riley held Evan's hand tight. "The castle and the pawns are the foundation of *the game*. Without them, no one survives."

Micah cleared his throat, making everyone jump. "I have the team's weapons."

"I know I'm the most unlikely game master, but I just wanted you to know," Riley added in a quiet voice. As she left with Kevin, Micah knelt down to look at her at eye level.

"If at any time Kevin tells you it's time to go, you listen to him and do as you're told," Micah said. "When *the game* is finished, then you and I will have a chat. Yes?"

Riley nodded her head in agreement.

Chapter 16

Rose and Robby greeted Micah as Kevin left with Riley to find her game room. Two vampiric guards, with eyes blazing red, begrudgingly carried in four large, wooden boxes. They placed them, one after the other along the metal and wooden benches of the team room and left. Micah looked at the human team comprised of misfits; a broken down All Star, a physical therapist dying of cancer, university professors, gun enthusiasts, and theologians and juvenile delinquents. He admitted to himself that they didn't have a chance.

"These are your weapons," Micah explained. "Modern adaptations from the original Roman version handed out at the last *game*. Each has been fitted with solar-infused, helio technology that's lethal to any vampire." He smiled, trying to give away as much confidence and reassurance as he could. He called the players by position.

George cleared his throat, looking concerned as he stood to ask, "There's hand to hand combat? I thought the chess move was called out, the pieces/players moved and..." He paused for a moment, realizing that he hadn't quite thought through the moment of a piece being taken. "Well, if it was a white side win," he said pointing to his uniform, "then the helio-bond threads in the black side uniforms would ignite, killing the beast...no offense."

Micah laughed. "None taken."

"And if it was a black side victory," George continued, "the vampire would merely bite the white piece's neck and it's over."

Micah sighed. He had hoped to avoid this conversation. "George, would you go to a hockey game to see the Red Wings play the Stanley Cup playoffs if you knew there wouldn't be a single punch or fight in the game?"

George thought about it and laughed, bleakly. He understood. Fighting was for show and entertainment. Neither humans nor vampires had evolved much since the time of Julius Caesar. Any game, especially this *game*, was sweetened by bloodshed.

"Pawns!" Micah called out with a type of enthusiasm not becoming an accountant. Evan and his seven other inmate companions stood up slowly.

Micah opened the first wooden box, lined with royal blue velvet and motioned for the boys to step forward. "The pawn is the foot soldier of *the game*. Here are your weapons." Micah handed each of the boys a huge bat.

Some of the boys looked at their weapon approvingly, swinging the bats in the air as if they were hitting a home run. Others appeared crestfallen.

"Rooks!" Micah called in his grandiose presentation. George and his assistant Eleanor stood and walked up to the box. "You two act as the castles and foundation of *the game*, protecting all of your team with your perimeter moves." He handed each of them long bundles of rope. Micah demonstrated how it might act to protect their bodies in defense. Conversely, it could strangle a vampire in an attack. Both of them looked skeptical as they walked back to their seats.

"Bishops!" Micah called. Two unlikely friends, Tom, a theology professor from the University of Detroit, and the other, Alan, a Rabbi from the West Bloomfield Jewish Community Center, stepped up. Micah opened the second box. He offered each of the men a cloth that wrapped around their shoulders, decorated with simple embroidery. In addition, they were each given daggers, one for each hand. Neither seemed to know where to put the long knives but still smiled at Micah gratefully.

"Knights!" Micah called. Robby nodded at two thick-armed men with shaved heads and they stepped forward. They each dwarfed him in size and height. Jack walked up first, an amputee from Iraq with a carbon and steel prosthesis. Given the choice between a double-sided axe or a bow and arrow set, he chose the compound bow. His fellow knight, Mike, was a member of the Michigan militia. He stared in disapproval at his two limited choices and chose a bow as well.

Finally, Micah opened the last box. He said nothing this time and the team looked towards their king and queen with subtle concern. Delicately walking to Rose, Micah handed her a pair of silk gloves decorated with similar embroidery as the bishops' mantles.

Rose looked back at Micah incredulously. "You're kidding right?"

Micah laughed. "Give me a moment. You'll see," he reassured her.

Returning to the box, he pulled out a beautiful broadsword, with etchings all down the blade.

"Bloody hell," Robby whispered as Micah handed it to him.

Micah backed away, looking slightly fearful. A loud click echoed off the cement walls, and suddenly the light in the room became nearly blinding due to all of the solar light radiating off the weapons and cloth.

"Your enemy may be one hundred times stronger, but these tools in your hands make you their equals," Micah said. "I'll be here with guards ready to protect and conceal your exit at the end of the first half of *the game*. Good luck." Micah hoped that no one could detect the sadness in his voice as he said farewell to his new friends. They were walking into a bloodbath of their own blood. It wasn't going to be like a hockey game. Hockey didn't even come close.

Evan stared at his solar-powered bat and laughed. "Equals my ass!"

Micah left the team and quickly made his way to where Riley was. *The game* was about to begin.

Care to place a wager? James texted.

You don't have any money, Ruth replied.

Something better than money? James persisted.

I'm listening, Ruth texted back.

James closed his eyes, listening to the crowd. He reached out with his mind to Quinn. His lover was dead, but James took a certain comfort in sending him mental messages anyway. "I'll be joining you soon. Then, I'll spend the rest of eternity making it up to you. If there's a place in the afterlife for the damned, I'll be with you soon."

James opened his eyes and texted Ruth. If black wins, I'll use my popularity as king to credit you, not the Council, for the wildly successful game. Then, I'll kill Jeremiah and Micah thanks to my numerous contacts. With the Council dissolved, you'll be ruler with my support.

Ruth typed, Who needs to bet on that? I've made sure that's exactly what's guaranteed to happen. I'm so happy to know I have you as my loyal servant.

James replied, growing agitated. So you won't mind letting me place the bet for the under dogs?

And what might that be?

I only want one thing, he typed. If white wins, you meet me at the end of the game. Hand-to-hand death match, just the two of us.

A death match? Ruth replied. Nothing would make me happier. But unfortunately, killing the trium-phant and beloved king of the game wouldn't be very good for my career. Tempting...very tempt-ing. But no.

Jeremiah entered the black team room and reached out with his mind to check on the team morale. Scenes of gorging on their human enemy, feeling young and strong, were the typical thoughts as the vampires suited up. Some were not happy with the helio-bond infused uniforms, but the chance to feast openly presented a far greater payout. It was worth the pain in the long run.

He turned his eyes to Geraldine. Her mind was far more intri-cate, making Jeremiah work through the tight network of protec-tive webbing. He had seen this sort of mental protection in spies and informants. Briefly, he saw a conversation. That was the unfortunate part. He could only see the two, Geraldine and Ruth. In the vision, Geraldine was clearly human; a memory then. He pressed her mind, straining to hear what the two were saying. Hadn't James brought Geraldine into this *game*? What did Ruth have to do with all of this?

Geraldine gasped like a mouse. She could feel Jeremiah prying into her thoughts and she began looking for him. When their eyes met, she slammed a mental thick metal door in his face. She bared her teeth under blazing eyes. Clearly she was hiding something.

James was intently talking with someone on his cell phone. Perhaps Jeremiah could find the answers to his questions while James was distracted. But before he could enter the king's mind,

Geraldine walked over and kissed him. The vampire team cheered.

Setting aside his phone, James rallied his teammates. "On to the feast!"

With little time and his chance to find answers quelled by the queen, Jeremiah had one last morale check on his list. Entering the small room, he found Cadel, arranging and rearranging his strategy notes. His tie was loosened from his shirt and he had removed his suit coat to free himself of any discomfort. Jeremiah was distraught to find his old friend in such a state, and standing on the precipice of *the game's* start.

Cadel's phone vibrated with a text message. He quickly grabbed it. Jeremiah, still probing Cadel's mind, heard the game master hope it was Maria. Instead, it was Ruth. Jeremiah could hear the words in Cadel's vulnerable mind as he read the text.

"I'm sure you know the lethal consequences if you lose to that brat. I've worked too hard to make this *game* an olive branch to the human world as well as a lesson to our own kind. I won't lose, hence, you won't lose. Are we understood?"

Jeremiah stepped back into the open door and closed it silently. He didn't need to hear Cadel's reply. Win or lose, it was clear to Jeremiah what needed to be done. A separate chess match had been taking place right under his nose. He had been a pawn to a very clever queen.

Every so often, a pawn makes it to the final row, he thought. Hurrying to the platform to announce the opening of *the game,* he stopped briefly to speak with a few new converts he'd recently met in Italy. "Are you available after tonight's portion of *the game?*" he asked Antonio. "Cadel and I would love to get together and maybe combine a little work with pleasure."

Antonio, a young vampire from Italy, was known in certain circles for his marksmanship. He looked a bit surprised through his gleaming smile. "Whose work? I'm no chess player."

"No, no, more like *your* work," Jeremiah replied, sounding a bit more hopeful as his time pressed down to a few mere minutes.

"The great thing about my work," Antonio laughed, "is that I love it and it takes me to very interesting places. I'm at your service, although, I have no idea why in the world you would need me."

"All in good time. I have a few more special arrangements to make. Then it's show time. I'll find you."

The lights of the stadium darkened, leaving the glowing hologram of the two chessboards over the giant field. Slowly, the two illuminated boards and their pieces merged and became one, with a grid marking letters and numbers on the sides. There was some applause. Then, Jeremiah, dressed in a Roman tunic and wig, just as he had dressed in the last *game*, began to speak over the stadiums sound speakers. The screen above the field displayed the images as he narrated.

"Welcome to the second vampiric human match; welcome to *the game*. Tonight, we bring you two sides of a board, two teams, all champions in their own right, led by their royals. For the human team we have your lovely queen, Rose McIntyre." A picture of Rose, from the photo shoot, hovered over the stadium. The human side of the stadium clapped. "And now, your king; New Zealand All Black rugby Champion, Robby Davies!" At the sound of Robby's name, both human and vampire sides of the stadium cheered and applauded. His smiling face hovered in the air for a few extra moments.

Rose jabbed Robby in the ribs as they watched from the team room. "Well look at you; even vampires like rugby."

Robby grabbed Rose unexpectedly and kissed her. To her surprise, he kept kissing her, and for a full minute, she wasn't in a converted meat packing house in Detroit. She wasn't about to step onto a field that would be the site of horrific murders. She was just in his arms, kissing Robby back.

When he pulled away from her, he looked straight into her face. "That was the one hundred percent right thing to say at the moment."

"With a kiss like that, I really hope I think of the right thing to say again," she quipped.

Jeremiah introduced the vampire team. "Delicate, seductive and your black queen for tonight, I give you, Geraldine Genet!" The vampire patrons erupted with applause. "Your king and master, James Bangor!" The vampiric side stood up, and while his head hovered over the stadium on the screen, James stepped out in person and waved to the fans. He gave a snarl when he found Ruth in her box seat. He sent her a mental note. "See, they love me. Too bad you'll never have my endorsement."

A self-narrated film began to play on the screen, interrupting Jeremiah's dramatic, Roman introduction. He looked to Micah from across the field, who looked just as bewildered.

Ruth's voice started, "It's true our societies have never really gotten along." A clip of an old, black and white Dracula movie danced across the screen, making everyone laugh. "Let this *game* be the chance to show both vampire and human alike that there must be balance and adherence to the rules. Senseless killing does not go unpunished." A clip of starving vampires within their cells in the *facility* projected on the screen. The stadium was silent. "The vampire world is about justice. Tonight we will show those of us who can't follow the rules that they will have to fight for their immortality. As a generous offer, we've invited a few brave human souls to compete in the hopes to join our ranks."

The screen showed a large, close-up of Ruth speaking to a crowd and the lights directed the audience to the live person as she stood center field.

"Thank you all for coming tonight. To demonstrate the idea of vampiric justice, I've personally worked closely with human authorities to apprehend one of the most notorious human criminals in their midst."

From a small television in a side room, Helen watched the opening ceremony as well.

Ruth continued to speak as a large cage slowly lowered down from the ceiling. "Selling drugs to small children, resulting in five deaths, more than two hundred counts of human sex trafficking and slavery, our vampiric and human authorities have worked together to apprehend this man."

Pictures of dead children, beaten women and mass graves glided across the screen.

"This is my dream. For our societies to work together for the betterment of our world." Ruth turned to Ray, who was protesting the accusations before him. "This is vampiric justice."

The floor suddenly dropped out from the cage at Ray's feet and he fell to the chamber below the field floor. Fifty starving vampires stared at Ray with hungry eyes. The cameras Micah had placed within the holding chamber now fed into the screen above the field. Hundreds of spectators watched as the feeding frenzy ripped Ray apart in under a minute. He never had time to scream, or run or think. While Robby watched from the team room with Rose at his side, and his team behind him, Helen ran to the door of her room only to find it locked from the outside.

Chapter 17

Riley clenched her fists to stop them from shaking as she stood at the large glass wall. She could see the stadium-size chess board below. She watched as her friends, dressed in white, carrying glowing weapons in their hands, stepped out onto the field. She watched the vampire side of the stadium erupt with emotion. Some raised their fists in the air, while others barred their teeth. One group, dressed in Victorian velvet dresses, donned opera glasses to get a better look. Her heart raced and she desperately wished that it was the vampires, not the human patrons, sealed behind the glass wall.

Kevin cleared his throat and pulled out her chair, inviting her to come away from the window and concentrate on the chess board.

A large camera was over her table. It would record her every move, and she reminded herself that she must never touch a piece if she didn't intend to play it. She thought of Robby and Rose. If she hesitated, it would only encourage the vampires in the audience. She had to stay focused. The gravity of the situation came crashing down on Riley as she peered over the bottom of the glass wall from her table.

The vampiric team stepped out onto the field. Even Kevin couldn't turn away as the black team lined up in formation. They were far more muscular. While the helio-bond-infused thread was meant to weaken them, from the audience perspective, the ambient glow gave them a god-like presence. There was absolutely no doubt who the under dogs were.

Kevin was convinced Riley would crack under the pressure. As she watched the two teams take their places, he thought she might burst into tears of hopelessness.

The vampire side could barely contain themselves. Jeremiah upped the voltage of solar power, sending it into the threads of the black team. A few began to smolder but it didn't stop the players from salivating and growling, many in a pounce stance. Some of the black team pawns egged on the white team pawns, extending their claws and describing agonizing deaths.

Robby looked behind him to see that the human audience was silent. He couldn't stand it. Stepping out of line, he put his sword down and walked to the line just in front of his pawns. Confusion and complaints came from both sides. Robby signaled to Riley for one minute. She nodded profoundly, even if he couldn't see her. He turned to his pawns; all the teenage boys' faces eagerly questioned their leader.

"Set down your bats, boys," Robby instructed.

Immediately feeling vulnerable, each of them protested.

Robby looked behind him at the crowd and then to the boys and screamed, "I said fucking do it. Now!"

The pawns moved quickly, setting their bats at their feet, shocked and afraid.

Robby tried to calm down. "Did you ever match moves with a hot girl on a dance floor?"'

All of the boys looked to themselves.

Evan was the first to answer. "What the hell kind of question is that at a time like this?"

"Well did you?" Robby insisted.

Evan shrugged. "Yeah, man."

"Well, this isn't anything like that, but match my moves and say what I say and be the biggest badass you can. Don't hesitate. Just do it...just like I do." He stood in front of the boys and puffed out his chest. Then he crouched and began to beat his hands on the tops of his tree trunk thighs. The boys looked at one another but copied his crouched stance and the beating of his legs. Soon,

Robby began pounding his chest while he stared straight into the
eyes of James. He began to shout,
Ringa pakia
(Slap the hands against the thighs)
Uma tiraha
(Puff out the chest)
Turi whatia
(Bend the knees)
Hope whai ake
(Let the hip follow)
Waewae takahia kia kino
(Stamp the feet as hard as you can)
Ka mate! Ka mate!
(It is death! It is death!)
Ka ora! Ka ora!
(It is life! It is life!)
Ka mate! Ka mate!
(It is death! It is death!)
Ka ora! Ka ora!
(It is life! It is life!)
Tenei Te Tangata Puhuru huru
(This is the hairy man)
Nana nei tiki mai
(Who fetched the sun)
Whakawhiti te ra
(And caused to shine again)
A upa ne ka upa ne
(One upward step, another upward step)
Upane, Kaupane
(An upward step)
Whiti te ra
(The sun shines!)

The boys matched Robby move for move, and soon one man leading a line of boys became one moving, ebbing, flowing unit of intimidation.

Robby turned to the human side of the stadium and yelled to them, "That's how you tell these buggers how to fuck off where I come from!"

The crowd cheered, many standing and clapping, others yelling insults to the other side of the stadium. On the vampire side, a few nodded their heads in approval at the bravery of the human team. As Robby walked to the back row of his team, he waved to the enthusiastic crowd, much like he had when he won the World Cup.

George gave him a broad smile and the boys picked up their bats with enthusiasm. Robby gave Riley a wave. She beamed with confidence. Kevin sat back in awe at how one man, in the face of such adversity, and staring death in the face, had found a way to rally a people in less than five minutes. He was thankful for Riley's sake. For the first time all night, the white team and its game master had hope.

Jeremiah, resuming his position of Master of Ceremonies, straightened his wig and puffed out his chest. With a wave of his hand he declared, "Let *the game* begin!"

Two images floated over the life-size board and its players. The first was the combined image of the two game master boards. The second was the view from the holding chamber below the board's grated floor.

As the rules dictated, white moved first, and the opening was all on Riley. She leaned into the small microphone dangling just below the camera and said, "E4."

On the field, the boy standing next to Evan saw the square at his feet illuminate. Then, the space just ahead of him also began to glow, showing him his new position. Tapping his solar-powered bat in the palm of his hand, he stepped forward and stood in his new square.

Evan could tell that standing closer to the enemy all alone was difficult. The muscles in the boy's back rippled in tension under his uniform.

Cadel spoke soon after. "C6."

It was a conservative move without any direct engagement. The vampire side booed at the anticlimax.

Riley took a deep breath and called her second player, "D4."

Evan felt his heart leap into his throat, followed by a throbbing in his head. The microbes hadn't left his body yet and it still instilled a panic reaction in him. Staring for a moment at his feet, he followed the path to the next glowing square to feel his stomach flip. He was to move closer to the enemy than the first pawn. Visualizing he was back on the street, he walked to the square and stared down the vampire across from him.

Vampire fans began to chant for blood. "First kill! First kill!" They stomped and clapped.

Evan stared up at them, his heart pounding in his chest.

Cadel baited the crowd by calling, "D5."

A huge vampire, three times Evan's size, began to charge, but fell short and to his knees just in front of Evan. Jeremiah was clearly keeping the vampire in line as the pawn began grabbing at his throat.

Evan could see the vampire's flesh bubbling under the red-hot collar. Evan took a small step back inside his square and the vampire fans cheered. In defiance, he and his fellow pawns crouched down and placed their bats across their chests as if to fight and defend themselves. The center of the board was the power point and Riley evaluated herself.

She looked to Kevin who put his hands up, "Go slowly," he tried to coach.

She looked ahead to the logical possible moves. Then, she called, "E5."

The first pawn to be called was being asked to move ever closer to the enemy. Both he and Evan had a writhing vampire next to them. The creature snarled and gripped at his collar, twisting and contorting in his square with blood so close and yet so unattainable until given permission by the game master.

Cadel wasted no time in calling his move, confidently. "Bishop F5."

From the back row of the black team came a wildly handsome vampire with wavy long hair. His glowing square was next to the pawns. When he arrived, he sneered at the small boy, who held his stance with his bat. As the vampire fans chanted louder, the bishop backhanded the white pawn in the square next to him. The crowd went wild. The boy gripped his face as he lay on his own square. A trickle of blood ran down his cheek. When the bishop noticed the cut he had made, he found a trace of blood on his fingernail. Waving it to the crowd, he then placed his fingertip to his lips and dramatically licked it. The move was effective and the crowd joined him in applause and mocking the wounded boy.

Robby righted his grip on his sword in anger. Rose bent to her haunches in order to calm down.

The bishop as well as Cadel noticed the psychological effect it was having on the human royals with a certain sense of satisfaction.

Riley stared at the chess board, trying not to let the drama of *the game* pull her away from deep concentration, but the noise and the antics of real live players bombarded her. But she had to stick to her plan. She placed her hands on either side of her head, and over her ears, and stared at the board. As she called out her move, the screen above the field recorded it. "Knight C3."

Mike, unable to contain his anger through the taunting, stepped out to his square with his bow and arrow drawn. The human fans cheered him on, countering by chanting, giving him the nickname, "Crossbow! Crossbow!"

Robby tapped his fingers nervously. One slip of Mike's finger on the crossbow trigger and an arrow would fly somewhere into the vampire crowd. If they were lucky, the solar-infused arrow would only maim the innocent bystander, but it would still be the death of them all. Robby wondered if the overzealous militia man could contain his need for revenge just a little longer.

Cadel seemed bored with Riley's move and yawned. "E6," he called out.

Another black pawn moved, this time in front of Evan and his fellow pawn. Face to face, the two opponents stared each other down as both sides of the stadium called for blood.

Riley pushed her chair away and walked around the board. The cement floor under her feet was vibrating from the enormous tension building in the stands. By the time she made it back to her seat, she called out, "Bishop E3."

Alan swallowed hard, realizing that it was his turn to head into battle. Looking across the way from his new square, he tried to give Mike a calming look. The knight was still aiming his bow wildly and it made Alan nervous.

Cadel called out soon after, his move indicating to Riley he was preparing for a kill. "Knight E7."

Riley decided to go in on the attack, sending her pawn up to challenge the black bishop, "G4." The human side cheered louder as the older boy took his place right next to the bishop and started to verbally taunt his enemy.

"Why don't you try smacking somebody your own size, motherfucker? I'll bash your head in with a bat full of sunshine."

To the huge disappointment of the vampire crowd, Cadel pulled back. "Bishop G6." Cadel could hear the crowd call out in protest while the human side laughed and jeered. His phone vibrated on the table next to the board; it was a text from Ruth.

Enough of this dramatic nonsense! You're making me look like a fool!

Cadel typed back. Us or you in particular? I'm testing my opponent. How dare you question my ability? Perhaps you'd like to come up here and take my place?

There was a long pause, and then the phone vibrated again. Dawn will be here before you know it. Get on with it.

Chapter 18

As the players moved and jockeyed for position according to their game masters, the hunger crazed vampires congregated under the white side of the field.

Rose tried not to move as gnarled fingers protruded through the grated floor. The vampires below roared for blood.

Robby shifted his weight and placed his heavy foot on some of the fingers within his square. The roaring became louder. The vampire fans cheered on the bloodthirsty inmates and chanted for blood.

Cadel, in his small room, could hear them through the glass. It was intoxicating for him to know he had all of vampire society in the palm of his hand. And yet, it was difficult to concentrate with the thought that Maria sat on the human side of the stadium.

Riley called out her move. "Knight GE2." As the second white knight was called out, a cheer from the human side could be heard. A group of men, wearing camouflage and black head scarves fist-pumped in the air. They continued to cheer as their man took his place standing in front of the queen to protect her.

Cadel recorded the move, then moved his perfect lips to the microphone and called out, "H5." A black pawn stepped out of formation with little consequence.

Ruth tapped her nails on the side of her cell phone impatiently.

Riley began to go on the attack. She called her militia man knight to move to center of the field, tempting Cadel into battle. "Knight F4."

More cheers came from the human side as others joined the militia members in their support.

Ruth looked at her watch. She wasn't sure how long she could endure the humiliation.

A low, deep laugh came over the stadium speakers. It echoed off the walls, creating a hush over the crowd.

"H-G4," Cadel announced.

All eyes were on the board as the lowly black pawn that seemed insignificant only a moment ago, walked up and plunged his long, yellow nails into the throat of the boy standing next to Evan. The vampire pawn lifted the boy off his feet as blood ran down and onto the grated floor. He held the boy up like a prize as the vampire spectators cheered and gave a standing ovation. Then, he pulled the boy's chest to his lips and plunged his teeth into the rapidly beating heart.

Evan wasn't sure what was louder, the roar from the one side of the stadium or the roar beneath his feet as the first drops of blood made their way to the holding chamber below.

Kevin looked concerned as he stared at Riley. She was emotionless. She stared at the board in deep concentration. He wasn't sure if he should feel alarmed or relieved at her disregard for the world outside the glass walls.

When the black pawn had finished drinking the boy's blood, he dropped the body onto the floor. Through the grates, the starving prisoners grappled for the scraps.

Evan watched the body flop like a fish out of water with activity as the fingers from below grabbed through the grates. After a moment, the body was carried away and *the game* continued.

Riley's voice was stoic as she called out, "Knight G6."

Kevin went to the glass wall to watch the militia man move into the thick of enemy territory. He looked back and stared at Riley disapprovingly.

Cadel wasted no time in calling, "Knight G6."

More shouts and cheers of elation for the vampires as a huge vampire knight leapt towards the white knight and kicked him in the face. The man went sailing onto his back with a hard thud, knocking the wind out of him. As he lay on the board, gasping for air, his hands shook as he tried to aim his bow at the giant towering over him. The vampire kicked away the weapon with ease. As the starving vampires ripped away at the clothes on the man's back, tearing away his flesh and draining his blood from below, the vampire knight bent down and plunged his teeth into the man's jugular, drinking deeply.

Ruth stood up to applaud the old school tactic and several others joined her in the adoration of her knight. When the body was carried away, the crowd waited.

Riley stared at the chess board in silence, the entire stadium holding its breath. From under her shirt, she pulled out a chain with a small locket. She opened it and stared at the picture of her father inside. Closing her eyes, she took a deep breath and leaned into the mic. "Queen G4."

While the vampires applauded, Rose swallowed hard. Robby grabbed her hand and stopped her from moving. He stared up at Riley in the glass box. Rose squeezed his hand reassuringly. There was no choice. If she didn't take her place, hundred of vampires would surely descend upon them in an uproar. She made her way to the square assigned.

"Knight D7," Cadel countered.

Kevin watched as Riley looked encouraged.

"Castle," Riley called out. In 'castling,' Robby's place was taken over by the rook, George, while Robby stood next to him at the left. Three pawns stood in front of Robby, forming a protective wall.

Ruth texted Cadel, his cell phone vibrating in his pocket. The text read: That's more like it. Keep the crowd going, Game Master.

Cadel leaned back in his chair in deliberation. He searched the human faces until he found Maria. He stared at the text from Ruth.

After several long minutes of staring at his board he announced, "Queen A5."

Walking like a runway model, Geraldine broke from the ranks and made her way to her square.

Riley whispered something to her locket, and as Kevin intently observed, in his scientific way he could see that Riley was talking to her father. She was asking for his help and asking questions much like they did when she had played chess with him when he was alive. Kevin wondered if Delta, in all of her quiet study, had ever followed chess. He sent her a plea for aid just in case. He opened his eyes when he heard Riley call, "Bishop D3."

More reinforcement surrounded Robby. He knew it was part of *the game* but he hated it. Rose stood out in the open, vulnerable, while he sat protected. For a man used to the physical full engagement of rugby, he began to feel emasculated.

Cadel jockeyed for positioning towards the center of the board. "Knight E7."

Riley smiled and sat on the edge of her seat. "Bishop G5," she called. She was on the attack again, even if only slightly formidable by way of a theology professor.

"B5," Cadel called, sending one of his pawns to protectively guard Geraldine. A bell chimed over the stadium, indicating there was one hour before the end of the first *game* night. Security would hold off the vampiric patrons for twenty minutes as a safety precaution, then all exits would be opened so that the rest could make it home safely before dawn.

Riley felt the pressure build. "King B1," she said, meekly.

Robby took one step to the left with a look of curiosity on his face. Rose gave him a reassuring smile from across the field.

Those from the holding area below who had not been lucky enough to feed from the two human kills, began to hang from the grates.

Evan could hear their jaws snapping open and closed in frustration.

Cadel built up his move, calling, "Knight B6."

Maria looked on as Cadel protected Geraldine with a power player. Maria shook her head in disapproval and Cadel could feel her disappointment.

Riley pushed her plan further, never breaking her concentration to look outside or at Kevin. "Knight E2."

The war veteran pulled back in retreat as he was told, giving the game master booth a loathing stare as he did so.

"Aha!" Cadel said, forgetting that his mic was so close. "Knight C4."

The vampire knight moved as close as he could to taking over Riley's vantage point.

Boos and hisses erupted from the human side at their game master. Riley hadn't given their side a kill, instead they had suffered two losses. Now, her knight was in retreat as dawn approached. She made a move to protect the knight.

Cadel pushed Riley harder, putting his most powerful piece closer to her king. "Queen B4."

Maria opened her mind to Cadel from across the way. "Kill her! Kill her now if you love me!"

Before Cadel could answer her, Riley called her next move, this time with more enthusiasm. "Knight B3."

The soldier ran to his illuminated square and stared Geraldine down, standing right in front of her.

There was a long pause as Cadel looked over his board. He clearly hadn't expected a rally before the end of the night by a small girl who was most likely up past her bedtime. He smiled at her tenacity. "Knight E5," he countered finally.

The human patrons cheered and hugged one another as the vampire knight retreated back.

Robby's heart leapt into his throat as Riley soon called out again, "Queen G3."

Rose took one step back.

Cadel advanced himself. "Knight C4," he said.

As the knight returned to Geraldine's side, Ruth complained to Cadel once more. We need something exciting for the end of this first night. Stop jostling the board and kill one of them! she typed.

Geraldine barred her teeth as she ran her tongue seductively over plump lips. "I've never tasted the blood of a soldier," she taunted.

Riley was in the middle of calling her move when the bell rang. "Rook HE1."

Jeremiah instructed Eleanor to move. When she was standing next to George, he waved a hand to offer Cadel one minute to make his final move. Seconds passed. The vampire patrons were anxious to leave as the dawn approached.

With eight seconds on the clock to spare, he called out, "G6."

A black pawn swiped at Alan's face, nearly knocking him over in a final gesture, making the vampires laugh.

Jeremiah stepped to the podium. "This concludes tonight's part one of *the game*. See you tomorrow for what will surely be an exciting conclusion."

As promised, Micah whisked the human team and their game master away in cars waiting just outside the stadium. Once inside the house, Riley went straight to her room and closed the door. Kevin quickened his pace to speak to her, but was stopped by Rose.

"She's been through a lot in the last few hours," she implored. "Let her sleep. You can talk to her tomorrow."

"The same could be said for you," Robby interjected, placing his hands on Rose's shoulders.

169

She made her way to the kitchen and poured a tall glass of water, then swallowed a handful of pills. Robby looked on. For someone so sick, she still had time to help if she could.

"That being done..." Robby refilled her glass. "It's off to bed with you." As he walked Rose to her room, he handed her the glass of water and turned down the hallway. Rose grabbed his arm, and saying nothing, she pulled him silently inside and closed the door behind them. Unzipping her uniform, it fell to the floor, revealing a thin but still athletic body. She made her way to him and wrapped her arms around his neck with a sigh.

"Last night on earth calls for better than that," he smiled. Removing his own uniform, he lifted Rose off her feet and placed her gently on the bed. Kissing her, she lay in his embrace, their bodies intertwined. He stared into her eyes and could see the exhaustion of the cancer that ate away at her from the inside. "Sleep," he whispered.

"What?" Rose asked, surprised.

"I'm not telling you no. I'm a man after all and there's nothing I want more. But there'll be plenty of time when you wake up. Besides, you might give me a run for my money and I need to be rested, too."

Rose smiled half-heartedly. She hated to admit that he was right.

He kissed her again. "I'm not going anywhere."

Ruth phoned the captain as she drove down Woodward. "Is everything prepared for our champions?"

"Exactly to your specifications, madam."

Helen tried to scream to whoever was on the other end of the phone. Naked and tied to a long banquet table, Helen's mouth was gagged to keep her quiet. A young woman, heavily-drugged, had been picked up minutes ago from the street. She sat slumped over a chair. The captain checked the arteries in the girl's neck. As he jostled her head, the girl argued, "I thought you brought me up here for a reason. I blow you and you give me the syringe. Let's get on with it."

The captain's phone rang again. It was Ruth. "We're here. Do it now."

As the vampiric team entered the room, one by one, Ruth led James and Geraldine in ceremoniously. "As promised, a feast. Captain?"

"We all know how you like your feasts...*seasoned*," the captain laughed. "To the king!" James quickly plunged the syringe into the girl's neck. He waited a few seconds for the overdose to run rampant as her pounding heart washed the drugs over her organs, tissue and saturated her blood. A flick of a long switchblade could be heard and the girl didn't flinch. Her eyes rolled back in her head as a faint smile danced across her lips. The captain lifted the small-framed junky over Helen and a guard took the switchblade. Slitting the girl's throat and chest cavity, the drug-filled blood poured out, all over Helen. She began to shake uncontrollably, realizing that she was the main course being basted in the juices of the heroin-laced life force of an addict off the streets.

Ruth smiled wickedly. "To the victors, go the spoils."

James was the first to jump at the chance. He could smell the two things he both loved and hated most in life. Ruth watched him closely, knowing by tempting him she was controlling him.

James took a deep breath and gained his composure. He took Geraldine's hand and the king smiled, standing at the end of the table at Helen's head. Though gagged, her eyes fiercely tracked James' every movement.

The king addressed his team. "My queen is new to our way of life and so if you'll permit me, I'd like for her to sample one of the delicacies of being a vampire." He didn't wait for a response. Instead, he turned to Geraldine, looking at her through hooded eyes as if he were about to seduce her. "Humans often eat things merely because they taste good. So it goes with vampires."

Without any warning, James quickly cradled Helen's forehead with his hands, and then plunged his index finger and thumb into her eye socket. The eyeball he removed had a light glaze of blood from the trauma. He licked it, savoring the drugs in the blood and the strangely-sweet taste of optic tissue. He popped the morsel into his mouth and smiled. "Care to partake in the delicacy?"

Helen was flailing under her constraints as she screamed into her gag.

Geraldine, for once, looked timid but nodded in agreement that she would try. Several of the players laughed.

Ruth sneered as she looked on.

James repeated the removal of Helen's other eye, this time, with more force to be sure that the eyeball was coated in a thick layer of blood.

Geraldine tentatively tasted it, giving James a pleasantly-surprised look. Then, she too, popped the eye in her mouth and enjoyed the treat.

James raised his hands to his team. "Please, join us!"

As the vampire team descended upon Helen, killing her slowly so they might enjoy the flavor of the captain's efforts and preserve the freshness of the blood, they kept her alive as long as possible.

Chapter 19

Antonio placed his black, canvas bag down on the hotel floor. He closed every curtain and blind in the hotel room. When he felt he was protected, he untied the front of his black turban and unwrapped his face cautiously. When he sensed no pain, he removed the cloth completely from his head and dialed his phone. "I'm in," he said.

"Can you see the covered window across from your room?" Jeremiah asked. "Our man was supposed to mark it in some way."

Antonio laughed. In block-shaped, primitive letters made from pieces of masking tape, the phrase, 'Bite me!' was on the window—a private inside joke from the human brave enough to join in the hit. Somehow, masking tape messages were completely commonplace in Detroit. If one couldn't afford minutes on their track phone, surely leave your message by whatever means was handy.

"Message received," Antonio said.

"Good. Check your phone. I've deposited half of the amount we discussed. The other half will immediately be deposited as soon as the job is done."

"Excellent," Antonio replied. In all honesty, he wasn't sure that killing the highest-ranking member of the Council was an upward career move. He wondered how many centuries he would have to hide out in the solitude of the Italian countryside. There was sure to be retaliation once they found out she was dead. Fortunately, money had been no object to those who wished her removed from the picture. He could live off the hit for a long time. He hung up and began to assemble his customized rifle. He paused every so often to peer out the window and across the alley to Ruth's hotel window marked by someone on the inside. He wondered if the person hired to break inside Ruth's hotel room was desperate or stupid. After a few moments of deliberation, he decided on a bit of both.

Zoe squealed in delight at the compliments Ruth bestowed upon her culinary masterpiece as the two chatted on the phone.

Ruth's voice echoed off the concrete walls, "Genius! If only there was a vampire magazine for food reviews, my darling girl, you'd be their poster child."

Zoe laughed. "The addict was young, which should have added a sweetness to her blood. You really can't find that flavor once a human has passed twenty-five. But the royals liked it?"

"The heroin junky was a nice touch considering the king's sordid past," Ruth flattered. "Now I must love you and leave you. I'm just arriving in the basement of my hotel. I really am surprised my cell reception has been so good in this godforsaken steam tunnel. Still, a 'soak in the soil' might do me some good before tonight's final match."

"Just wait till you see what I have lined up for the championship feast," Zoe beamed on the other end.

"Something unforgettable, no doubt. Now, I'm off." Ruth hung up and took the service elevator from the basement up to her penthouse hotel suite. With the swipe of her key card, she hesitated at the door, searching for any ray of daylight sun that might have gone unchecked by her personal staff. The room was completely dark.

Closing the door behind her, she detected a musky smell coming from her bedroom. Her senses pricked and the hairs on the back of her neck stood on end with excitement. Her eyes tracked the human in the dark, lying in her bed. For a moment she wasn't sure if she should be furious or grateful. It had been a while. The muscular man pulled the covers away from his body, presenting her with a physique of near perfection.

"How did you get in here? Which of my staff did you pay off?" Anger was replacing curiosity. "This breech of security will not go unpunished."

The man lit a single, long-stemmed candle next to the bedside, letting the low light form flickering shadows across his chest. "I'm a gift of gratitude sent from the Council in Milano. They're very much enjoying *the game*," he added in a thick Italian accent.

"What makes you such a prize?" Ruth questioned, her temper rising but quelled by piqued interest.

"My family has been bred for centuries by the Milano Council. We're at their service in the hopes that our new master may find us worthy of eternal life and youth. In exchange, the Council has bred us with only the strongest, most beautiful and healthy of families in Italy, making me and my family a proper gift for only the most discerning recipient."

Ruth's eyes followed the chiseled contours of the man's body. He was the finest human specimen she had ever seen; she had to admit that. But as tempting as it was to think of drinking his blood until his body ran dry, there would be plenty of time for that later. Still, someone had just sent her the equivalent of a Lamborghini and he begged to be test driven.

"Do you have a name?" Ruth asked, taking off her silk blouse and pants.

"No. That's for you to decide. It's part of the honor of me being a gift and you being the recipient."

Ruth joined him in bed and ran her fingers along his torso. "Surely, you must have been called something these last twenty years."

"I'm a number and a letter. All of my family members are named with a combination of both. It's a daily reminder that I'm alive for a sole purpose. When referred to, I am Eleven T."

Ruth laughed and stretched out on the bed in her lace panties, her perfect breasts shaking slightly under her growing amusement. "Well, it's very clear to me that you were bred for your beauty and not your brains. In Roman numerals, your name is XI-T....or Excite. Do you understand?" She laughed, searching his face for enlightenment. Instead, he leaned over and kissed her.

"And do I? Excite you? My Council will want to know that their gift was appreciated."

"Let's find out..."

Antonio assembled the rifle and wiped it down clean. Buttoning the insulated collar of his shirt tightly, he picked up his turban cloth and wrapped his head and face completely. Over his eyes, he added thick welding goggles. Custom made, leather gloves, resembling tight driving gloves shimmied over his fingers. He took a deep breath to steady his nerves, then opened the small metal case next to the bag. As he lifted the lid, a blinding light filled the room as if he had just opened a box containing the sun. In essence, he had done just that.

Antonio opened the chamber of his rifle and placed the blazing bullet inside. He closed the chamber and waited for the signal. Through the metal of the gun, as well as his gloves, he could feel the heat and solar intensity of the helio-based ammunition. If the target took too long, he would be too weak to carry out the hit. Antonio counted the minutes impatiently. He could only stay so long before the mission would have to be aborted.

Ruth noted that she really must thank the Milano Council for their generosity. They had laid sexual perfection at her feet. As he drove that same perfection between her thighs, she felt herself begin to lose control, a very rare reaction for her with any lover. It was as if he could read her mind, or maybe her body, as he slowed and sped up, slowed and shifted position, bringing her close to orgasm and tapering her back to a deeper sense of wanting. Just as she found herself wanting to beg for release, she flipped him onto his back and regained control. Her lover seemed to enjoy the change as his moans grew louder.

Their pace was slow at first but Ruth, having been driven so close to the breaking point, refused to wait any longer. She quickened the pace, driving them both to the precipice. The man below her gripped her hips. He began to yell, inspiring Ruth to drive him harder. Beads of sweat ran off his abs and then came the release. The next minute passed in slow motion.

Everything in the room became silent for Ruth. She knew her lover was calling for her in the throws of his ecstasy. She watched him throw his head back and grind his teeth, but she couldn't hear him.

While in her orgasm, the window behind the thick curtain at the head of the bed shattered, and a blinding light exploded outside of her as well as within her. There was an old familiar sensation. She felt heat for the first time in forever within her chest.

Her mind searched through hundreds of years and thousands of stored mental images and feelings, until it found what it was looking for. The memory of death. At the moment her human self had died decades ago, the impression of death had traded places with her vampiric self. Her mind had never forgotten. Death had its own unique feeling, taste and smell. The last thing she saw was a robed figure, completely covered and concealed in the blinding light of the helio-infused ammunition glowing inside her body. The figure had Jeremiah's voice, which she heard say, "Confirmed kill."

By the time Antonio had received the confirmation, he was already in the safety of the blackened glass of Cadel's limousine, just outside the hotel. "I hope that I've served you well, Game Master."

"Chess, like real life, has its queens. They are the hardest to kill because they're the most powerful," Cadel said. "You've just made life better for all of us and served me very well. I must thank you for going above and beyond. He pushed a button on his phone. "The second half of your money has just been sent to your private bank account. I take it you'll be going into hiding for quite some time?" Cadel asked.

"Yes, Game Master. I've a hidden but lovely villa. It's sparsely staffed but plenty for my needs and very comfortable." Antonio smiled. "It has a breathtaking view of the sea under moonlight."

"Sounds lonely," Cadel said, surprising Antonio. Cadel turned his phone around, revealing a picture of Maria.

"She's more beautiful under moonlight as well," Antonio agreed. "Very beautiful indeed, Game Master."

"This is the love of my life," Cadel said. "I bought her from the Mafia as a girl standing on the edge of womanhood. It was my full intention to save her for a springtime feast, but she proved far more than I could imagine. She understood what I was and helped to bring me meals I wouldn't have had working alone. She proved herself smart and immune to my bloodlust. All the death that surrounded her night after night never hardened her. She's by far the gentlest creature I've ever known."

Antonio laughed. "Sounds like you should turn her and then marry her."

Cadel exhaled a jagged breath. "After all these centuries as a pure, moral vampire, I must admit I'm nothing more than a lowly man. I've betrayed her in the worst possible of ways. While I know that in time she'll forgive me, I can never forgive myself. I still lust for another. I don't deserve her."

Antonio stared speechless at the grand master. He had no idea what to say. Cadel, looking older than he had just five minutes earlier, stared up into Antonio's face and then took the assassin's hands. "Her name's Maria. She'll be sitting on the human side tonight. Find her. Tell her I sent you. Take her to your villa and turn her. I must know that she'll be well-cared for and loved as I would have loved her, had I truly been deserving of her." Cadel wore the look of desperation in his eyes. "Will you do this for me? I must have your word, in case something happens to me. I must know my Maria is safe with the only man alive who can protect her from human and vampire alike."

Antonio stared at the picture of the fresh-faced, girl next door. He deliberated on the right words. "Life truly is a strange thing. I'm not sure I deserve such a gift from such a great man as yourself, but I promise you, I'll love her and keep her safe."

"I want you to leave with her tonight. Don't wait to see the outcome of *the game*."

"Sir?"

"You'll understand in time. Will you agree?" Cadel pressed.

"Yes."

"And you'll safely turn her?" Cadel asked, staring back at the picture in his phone, unable to look at Antonio any longer.

"I will have her call you when the change is complete. You'll be able to hear it in her voice. Then we'll vanish. I have your word you won't come looking for her?"

Cadel paused and took a deep breath. "Yes."

"Then consider it done."

The game master shook hands with the assassin, sealing Maria's fate without her knowing.

Jeremiah jumped into the car, startling them both.

"She held on for a few minutes after the bullet penetrated her chest," Jeremiah scolded Antonio. "But the body's been disposed of and the servant turned. If the *gift* survives the transformation, he's been instructed to report to the Milano Council. We'll see. It was an awful lot of work and expense for the death of one vampire."

Cadel sighed. "Sometimes, several lesser pieces must position themselves and work together to take down one more powerful. Let us see how the game plays out tonight."

As the setting sun turned the sky from burnt orange to purple, Robby woke Rose with a cup of tea at her bedside.

Groggy and heavy with sleep, Rose blinked hard and sat up slowly. She frowned. "You're dressed?"

"You should be, too. We leave in half an hour."

Rose sulked and was going to protest when she was interrupted by Robby's mouth on hers. He kissed her so deeply that she melted back into the pillows.

"You needed the sleep more than you needed anything else. We'll have eternity after tonight."

Tears welled up in Rose's eyes. "What if we don't?" she whispered, then paused, trying to hold back the flood of tears. Her lips trembled. "What if we lose?"

"We won't. I won't let us lose." He kissed her again. "No more talking. Drink up and get dressed. Take your medicine and eat your Wheat Bix."

"I don't like breakfast or cereal."

"Save your strength and eat a steak then because after tonight, what I have planned for you and this bed is going to take at least a week." He flashed her a smile that no one in the world could resist and couldn't be argued against.

Thirty minutes later, the human team silently packed into the cars waiting outside. None of the boys playing pawn positions dared make eye contact with Riley.

George, nor Alan, seemed able to look at the girl without scowling. Robby touched Riley's shoulders and steered her in the direction of their car, where Rose was waiting.

As the car pulled away, Rose opened her bag and passed out vitamin water and sandwiches.

As Robby inhaled his hungrily, Riley stared solemnly at the locket around her neck. "They all hate me. The whole team. Who can blame them?" she said in tears.

"They don't hate you. They're just scared," Rose said, trying to reassure her.

Robby was less nurturing as the car turned the corner. The Detroit Meat Packing house was in sight. "Eat," Robby commanded. "Then, give your team a reason to be brave tonight. We all know you can do it."

Chapter 20

Riley stared at the chess board in front of her but her mind was somewhere else. It wasn't in the steel and concrete room with the large glass window in front looking out onto the spectators milling into the stands. Instead, her mind had drifted to a memory in the past. The room in her mind was sparse but safe in her father's apartment. When her parents had divorced, Riley's father had gotten an ultra modern loft within walking distance of the Wayne State. Her mother had called it cold, but Riley could see that the lack of things, the starkness, helped her father to think clearer. There were fewer distractions. Still, he had made sure Riley had her own room, filled with stuffed animals, a soft bed, a desk, and a case full of books.

In this particular memory, her father was reading softly to her. " 'And Alice said, I wonder if I've been changed in the night. Let me think. Was I the same when I got up this morning? I almost think I can remember feeling a little different. But if I'm not the same, the next question is: who in the world am I?' "

"Ah, that's the great puzzle!" At that her father had laughed lightly. He'd caught her again with her eyes closed. Riley tried to convince him to read more but he refused.

"You're falling asleep!" he said.

"No I'm not," Riley argued. "I'm just listening with my eyes closed."

"Oh, is that what you're doing? It looks a lot like sleeping. Besides, Riley, you're getting too old for your dad to read to you. You should read your own books."

"I do read my own books; when I'm with Mom, and when I'm at school. I read loads of stuff. I just like it when you read to me. I like the sound of your voice." A small lump grew in her throat as she added, "It makes me feel like, well, it just makes up for all the time when you're away. When you read to me, it's just you and me. You don't read to anyone else. So that's something that's all mine."

Her father kissed her forehead and turned out the light. When he drove her back home the next day, she found a box with a cell phone in it with a note that read, "If you want to hear the end of the story, call me at seven tonight. Tomorrow, we pick a new book. Love, Dad."

She longed to call him now and ask him for his help. She had most certainly changed overnight. *But if I'm not the same, then the question is: who am I?* she wondered and replayed her father reading aloud. She had gone down the rabbit hole and could see there was no way back. Riley thought of her team and her friends on the field.

Jeremiah announced the beginning of the second night. The vampire side of the stadium was fired up. They had left the stadium with the odds in their favor.

Both teams were announced and found their previous positions on the chess board. Hungry inmates below the floor gripped onto the metal grates and swung like animals. They snapped their jaws under the human team members' feet and taunted them, saying things like, "Tasty, tasty! It's dinner time!"

Riley was the first to move and she was cautious. She leaned into the mic and said, "C3."

One of the boys grabbed his bat and moved to the square straight ahead. He looked up into the glowing red eyes of the vampire knight. The monster stared down at him, grinning, baring his jagged, elongated teeth.

Cadel shifted in his chair and called, "Queen D6."

Geraldine turned and blew a kiss up to the game master as she took her position safely behind the fighting line. While it didn't inspire applause from either side, several laughed at the vampire queen's playfulness.

Riley wrote down the move and called out, "Bishop F4."

Micah watched from just outside Riley's box and cringed. The girl had played better chess against him in the wee hours of the night than she was now. He wondered if she was cracking under the life and death stakes. The move put Alan in the lethal reach of Geraldine.

Crouched and ready to pounce, Geraldine ran her tongue over her pearly teeth to inspire fear. Alan wrapped the helio-infused cloth around his neck and took a bracing stance. The vampiric side called for a kill, while the human side wrapped their arms around themselves, preparing for another loss.

Geraldine waited impatiently, glancing back at Cadel through the glass wall. She could smell the fear coming off the human bishop and her bloodlust was becoming unbearable.

Finally, Cadel leaned into his mic and called, "Queen D8."

The human side leapt to their feet with applause.

Micah upped the voltage charge in Geraldine's uniform as a warning to retreat back to the royal line. Personally, he breathed a sigh of relief. He wasn't sure why Cadel was toying and torturing his own queen and he didn't care. All he could hope for was an epiphany by Riley, and soon.

"Knight C5," Riley said quickly, pushing the game forward without waiting for the crowd.

Micah leaned forward as Riley moved in for some kind of attack.

"Bishop H6," Cadel countered. Most of the crowd on either side was still discussing the unusual break in the game with the retreat of the vampire queen to notice the game was picking up.

"Knight E6," Riley pressed.

Micah took out his phone and texted Kevin. `Is she crazy? She hasn't taken a piece yet and she's going straight for the queen?`

Kevin read the text and stared at Riley in the small room. He texted back, `She's moving and recording her moves faster than I've ever seen.`

`Is she cracking under the pressure?`

`Not sure,` Kevin replied.

The two were interrupted by screams of horror from the human side of the stadium as Cadel called, "FE6."

A vampire pawn jumped diagonally to grab the human knight with one hand. Before the knight could retaliate and fire his bow, the vampire pawn plunged his fist into the man's chest and ripped out his heart. The muscle was still pumping as the vampire sunk his teeth into it. The floor of the stadium thundered as throngs of starving inmates below basked in the blood that poured from the knight's chest cavity and through the grates in the floor.

Micah texted Kevin again. `She's caving.`

`What do we do?` Kevin asked in desperation.

Spectators from the human side stood and gaped as the knight's body was dragged away, the muscles of his hands, perpetually clenched around his weapon.

Micah texted back, `Do you believe in God? Now might be the time to start praying.`

Riley seemed unfazed and said, "Rook E6."

Placing George in the same place that his teammate had just fallen, he struggled not to slip on the square now thick with blood. The human side booed and hissed at their game master.

Cadel deliberated, then called out over the speaker, "Clever girl, but you'll need to work harder to distract me. Bishop F4."

Evan recognized the move immediately as an elegant street move. From the side, and appearing out of nowhere, came Cadel's bishop. Alan never knew what hit him. Avoiding the solar-powered protective cloth around his neck, the vampiric bishop leapt high into the air and plunged his teeth into the top of Alan's skull. Holding him by the lower jaw, the bishop drank the blood from Alan's brain and left the corpse. As the guards dragged the body away, the face and head were bleach white, the eyes sunken and glazed.

"Down the rabbit hole," Riley whispered into the mic. "Down the rabbit hole." The audience looked all around in confusion. Then Riley said, "Queen F4."

Micah looked up wildly and fumbled for his remote.

Rose stared at Robby desperately. She watched his chest heaving in panic and frustration. As Rose got closer to the vampire bishop, her gloves began to glow brighter and brighter. By the time she reached his square, the vampire was shielding his eyes and stumbling backwards.

Micah's thumb hovered anxiously over the button of the bishop's helio-bond suit. He had to make it look as though Rose were killing him with her gloved hands alone. As soon as she reached the bishop, Micah pressed the button to full voltage. The monster crumbled to his knees, smoke billowing from every millimeter of his suit as his flesh melted off his bones.

Rose continued to squeeze his throat as he thrashed and jerked, cooked alive in his uniform. Only when his lower torso disintegrated did she finally let go. She stood with tears streaming down her face. She exhaled in relief but no one heard her.

The human side finally had a kill. Micah breathed a sigh of relief and released the voltage. He made a call to the captain, putting on extra guards to protect the sealed-off human side. The vampiric patrons were going to be angry. The crowd had to be controlled.

Cadel studied his notes and stared at the chess board. He spoke somberly into the mic. "Rook F8." A very large vampire took his place next to Geraldine. Part of Cadel hated himself for being so protective of her. He knew he couldn't bear to see her burn. His only solace was that Maria was not in the audience to see his overprotection of a queen or his misplaced devotion.

Riley continued her rampage by using Rose. "Queen G5," she called out.

Robby worried when he heard Rose called upon again. He was happy for the small triumph but Rose was too weak to keep the pace. Suddenly, he was truly aware that his queen might die before he told her his true feelings for her.

Rose took her square directly in front of a lowly pawn. She clapped her gloves together in a feeble attempt at intimidation. The pawn laughed.

"King D7," Cadel said.

A hush fell over the vampire side of the stadium as James was asked to move out from the relative safety of the eighth row.

Riley looked up from her deep concentration and turned to Kevin. "This is the beginning of the end game. Tell Micah." She said it with such direction and authority that Kevin hesitated.

Riley didn't wait. She returned to *the game* and her resolved focus, forming her final line of defense. "Rook DE1."

Cadel moved similarly. "Rook F7."

Spectators from both sides of the field leaned in, sitting on the edges of their seats, speculating in whispers.

"B3," Riley said into the mic, sounding a bit like a small mouse.

"Knight B6," Cadel countered as he quickly moved his knight out of the way. The boy pawn looked disappointed as he smacked his bat on the bottom of his shoes.

"Bishop G6," Riley called.

The soft-spoken college professor hesitated. Staring at the glowing square across the field, the game master intended for him to protect Rose. But his short time in studying chess had still made a large impact; he could see his own demise. Staring the very high possibility of death in the face, he froze with fear.

The vampire side of the stadium laughed and yelled out, "Move!" and "On to glorious death!" It was followed by more laughing.

Riley called the move again as vampiric guards across the field began to assemble in formation.

Robby yelled at the top of his lungs, "If you don't take your chances in *the game*, the guards have the right to come and kill you on the spot. Now move!"

Rose motioned to hurry up and Jeremiah talked to the captain of the guards.

Riley called the move a final time and this time the bishop took his place, running to the illuminated square in front of Rose.

With an uncensored chuckle, Cadel announced his move. "Knight G6."

The vampire side of the stadium burst into fits of laughter as they watched the timid man become a meal for the knight. Ripping him to shreds, the already well-nourished knight donated most of the professor's blood to the inmates below the grated floor.

The holding chamber cameras showed scenes of the inmates bathing in the man's blood. Some of them even rolled in the runoff that oozed into the drains in the cement floor.

Rose closed her eyes as she was overtaken by a fit of coughing. Induced by weakness and the stress of watching a terrified man brutally murdered directly in front of her, she fought for control.

Riley pushed the timing of *the game* and called, "Queen G6."

"Bloody hell!" Robby shouted as Rose gritted her teeth. Thanks to the knight's surprise, Rose lunged for his feet, successfully knocking him down. Micah cranked up the voltage as Rose gripped the vampire's groin.

Between the activated helio-bonds of the suit and the concentrated energy of Rose's two gloves, the knight burst into flames at the torso. He screamed, trying to pat out the flames as he smoldered everywhere else.

Rose jumped back just in enough time to avoid catching herself on fire as the flames ignited all over him. When he was dead, the guards dragged the corpse away, the blackened body crackling the entire time. Rose took his square and lay down to rest within its small borders.

Robby could do nothing as he watched Rose slip away a piece at a time.

Micah checked his watch. There was still three hours before the dawn bell. Patrons on both sides stared at the human queen with sympathy. She was clearly dying, yet fighting it bravely. She coughed uncontrollably and blood sprayed across the square, igniting interest in the inmates below her. Finally regaining control, Rose slowly stood up. Both sides of the stadium applauded her determination.

Cadel wasn't as impressed. "Queen G8," he called, interrupting the adoration of the human queen.

Only one free square lay between the two most powerful pieces on the board as Geraldine took her place. The room seemed to hold its breath waiting for Riley.

When her voice echoed over the speakers, several people jumped, "Rook D6."

George stood in front of James and stared at him boldly.

"King C7," Cadel countered.

James took one step to the side, taking him out of danger. George tried to think of his research and all the good he would do with eternity. It helped him to be brave.

"Queen E6," Riley said, writing down her moves and whispering to her invisible father.

Rose gave George a reassuring smile as she stood beside him. He tried to smile back but it was clear from his forced expression that she looked as terrible as she felt.

"King B7," Cadel said, recording the move and counting ahead to his planned win.

James took one more step to the side, giving a wider distance between himself and Rose. The two teams were nose to nose. The smell of death, decay, cooked flesh and rusty, salty blood filled the ill-ventilated stadium.

Evan was tired and hungry despite the stench.

Riley counted and recounted. The players waited impatiently and Kevin began to tap his foot as Riley took her time.

"Dad, you're right!" she beamed and the audience looked up to the box. "I mean, Rook C6."

Trembling at the thought, George swallowed hard and then looked back at Eleanor. She waved her hands as if to tell him to go on. "I'm terribly sorry," he remarked to the wild-eyed vampire. "Your death is not in vain. It's all in the name of advancing science." It was his eternal dedication to science that helped George to murder the vampire. As the solar energy penetrated the undead body in waves and in particles, George wondered how many other countless lives had been sacrificed over the centuries in the advancement of knowledge.

Cadel seemed worried as he struggled to regain his power and domination of the board. "Queen H7."

Geraldine advanced the side of the board without drama or consequence.

Riley smiled at Kevin and leaned into the mic. "King A1."

Kevin walked over to the chess board.

Riley placed her small hand over the mic and whispered, "My father showed me. Look, we're going to win!"

Kevin watched Riley's board as Cadel made his move.

"Rook F2," he announced.

The sleek female vampire ran head on at one of the boys still standing in the pawn line since the beginning of *the game*.

The boy swung his bat in self defense but she ducked. Leaping into the air, the rook gracefully extended her long nails. The fingernails, combined with her immense strength, cut the boy's head clean off his shoulders. A look of surprise was forever cast on his face as the boy's head rolled past Robby. The torso eventually dropped to the floor, the main artery spurting out with each compression of the still-beating heart. The rook drank from the torso like a drinking fountain. The vampire side of the stadium cheered in victory.

Robby's stomach rolled and he had to look away, but he was quickly sucked back into *the game*.

"Queen D6," Riley called.

As Rose made the short jaunt, Kevin tried to make heads or tails of the win Riley so confidently boasted.

Cadel was ready and countered, "Rook F7."

Rose looked to her right nervously. It felt like she and George were being surrounded. If they were about to die, she hoped Riley would give her one last attack on Geraldine. The vampire queen would be sure to kill Rose quickly; she looked hungry.

Micah burst through the door, his eyes immediately on Riley. "Don't move until you see it. Count it. It breaks the rules to tell you, but you've got him in six."

Riley looked up from her board with an annoyed expression. "Get security ready. I have him in four." She sighed. "We'll only need one car though."

"Are you sure?" Micah asked desperately. He looked out onto the field, wondering who, besides the king, would be left alive.

"I'm sure," Riley replied. "Dad's never wrong."

Micah glanced at Kevin as if to ask, but decided it wasn't the right time. Instead, he looked to Riley once more. "Can you do it before the sun comes up? You have just under an hour before the dawn bell."

Riley rubbed her necklace and took a deep breath. "One car. Be ready. *The game* ends now."

Chapter 21

The countdown to the ringing of the dawn bell clipped away fragments of time. There could be no hesitation in any of Riley's moves or concentration. The sun was coming. Her queen was dying, and an entire stadium held its breath waiting for the conclusion of *the game*.

"Rook E6," Riley announced.

Eleanor took her place on the other side of Rose. The two women smiled at one another, trying not to give up.

"Rook D7," Cadel called out.

Riley looked to Kevin. "I'm pretty sure at this point that Cadel still thinks he can win. He has Rose, George and Eleanor all surrounded." She looked to Micah, her hand still covering the mic. "That's where he's wrong. My father had told me to remember that anything that can implode can also explode." Micah stared at the chess board, nodding in agreement at her statement.

Leaning into the mic, Riley said, "Rook B6."

George was sent to attack the knight to his left. He was tired and his rope wasn't as effective as he'd hoped on the vampire. Evan threw him his bat in a desperate attempt to help him, and George found his courage, bashing in the knight's head, all the while screaming, "One for the many!"

Robby held up his hands and began yelling to the audience, rallying the tired, living spectators. The human patrons began to chant with him, "Saint George! Saint George!" The cheering worked. The vampire was dragged away, and for a moment, George and his eternity of dedication to medical cures for humanity came within his reach. He waved to the fans and smiled. But he would never see his work save the masses.

Cadel retaliated and called, "AB6."

A lowly pawn from the side of the board disemboweled George with several slices of his talons across George's midsection. The vampire crowd cheered when the pawn refused to deal the final blow to end George's life. Instead, the pawn insisted that George slowly suffocate and bleed to death. George lay in agony, unable to speak, gasping for air under the collapsing of his diaphragm.

Rose called out for the pawn to finish him off but Jeremiah announced it was a fair, albeit slow kill. He insisted *the game* continue. All the while, George was on his knees, his blood slowly seeping into the floor. Gravity pulled at his viscous intestines. The vampires below poked their claws through the grates and tore away at the oozing organs. He stared at Rose and Eleanor in horror.

"Queen B6," Riley called. With her adrenaline pumping, Rose wanted nothing more than to kill the pawn torturing George. She took the rope from George's trembling hands, and breaking into a full run, she leapt towards the pawn. She landed right in front of him and stuffed the rope in his mouth with her helio-gloves. The pawn's head burst into flames within seconds.

Rose cried tears of anger and frustration. Killing the pawn still hadn't spared George a slow and agonizing death. She looked back to the eighth row and found Robby. He looked shocked and she wondered if he might ever think the same of her. He now saw that she was capable of revenge and murder. They both knew that now.

Rose looked to her game master and shouted, "Finish it!"

As the guards dragged the flaming pawn away, Rose broke rank and went to George. He sat with his hands clenched around his exiting organs. His lips were turning blue from lack of oxygen. She wrapped her arms around his neck; just like she'd watched the vampires do in *the game*. "I'm so sorry," she cried, kissing George on the cheek. In an act of mercy, she broke the professor's neck.

Robby stared hard at his queen from across the chess board. Their eyes met. She watched his expression and wondered if he might ever see her in the same loving way again. Was she too much of a monster, even under these tremendous circumstances, for him to love?

"Queen B6," Riley said.

Micah texted the guard to bring a car. Fifteen minutes remained to the dawn bell. The guard didn't reply back. Micah whispered to Kevin, "I don't think the plan was for you to win."

"I seriously doubt there will be a car waiting for us unless it's to take us to the nearest back alley for them to feast on us," Kevin surmised.

Cadel moved James as far away as he could from Rose. "King C8," he said.

The vampire side of the stadium were on their feet, applauding their game master for protecting his king.

Micah pulled Kevin closer. "I'm afraid the opposition will jump onto the field and kill you all." He checked his phone. Still no response. "I have a backup plan. As soon as Riley calls her last move, get her next door to the church. I'll have all of the windows open. No one will dare chase you for fear of the sun."

"What about you?" Kevin whispered frantically.

"I have to get the champions to safety." Micah smiled and in a blink, vanished.

"Rook E8," Riley said and Eleanor moved to the eighth row, trapping James.

Cadel sat staring at the board.

"Checkmate!" Riley yelled.

Jeremiah checked and re-checked the players on the field. The human side of the crowd had burst into applause and cheers. They jumped up and down and jeered the other side from the relative safety of their sealed-off glass enclosure.

Micah made it down to a small room just off the locker room. "Run! In here, now!" he called to Robby and the last remaining players on the human team.

Eleanor, the farthest from the point of safety, began to run, but Geraldine was faster. She pounced on Eleanor's back, knocking the woman to the bloody grates that were the floor. She screamed as Geraldine began to tear away the back of her uniform.

Rose heard Eleanor and stopped running. Turning around, she considered going back. A rage inside her battled her weakened state.

A riot was erupting on the vampire side of the stands. The undead fans were livid about losing.

When Robby made it to the door that Micah held open, he turned to grab Rose. "What the hell is she doing?" Robby asked Micah in a panic.

Evan jumped into the secure side room and his feet didn't stop until he collided with the cement wall. "They're gonna kill us! We fucking win and now they're gonna kill us anyway!"

Micah looked up into the vampire crowd. He dialed his captain and shouted into the phone, "If you ever want peace in this century, make sure the human patrons are sealed in. They just have to wait a few more minutes until dawn. Protect the locks!"

Robby ran towards the approaching sea of claws, ignoring the vampires that rushed the field like a tidal wave. He wondered if his eyes were playing tricks on him. The faster he ran towards Rose, the quicker she ran towards him. Eleanor must surely be dead but how was Rose running towards him so quickly? Closer. Faster. Closer.

Robby stopped for a split second as Rose was about to run him over. Soon, he was flying as fast as she was. When he looked around, he nearly punched James in the face.

"She's dying!" James shouted. "I can smell death on her!"

"In here!" Micah called to the three of them. He dared not tell them about the sweeping tsunami of death that was about to engulf them if James didn't run just a little bit faster. The vampire mob was running towards any human that they could take out their revenge on, and they wouldn't stop to spare a moment to tear apart a fellow vampire to get to them.

Robby heard the door shake like thunder as the wave of bodies collided with the locked door of their room. Inside the small room, the boom sounded like an explosion as a moving force of charging vampires collided and jumped at the glass walls of the human area just above them. But then celebrating inside the glass enclosure abruptly halted, as human patrons watched the charge headed straight for them.

The vampires leapt onto the glass walls and pounded their fists, stomped their feet, and raged for blood. Like ants on a dead animal, they plastered the glass on all sides, looking for weak points in the seals, checking for the locks, clawing and slashing at the thick glass barrier.

"So who made it back?" Robby shouted over the noise, as he looked around the room, trying to catch his breath. He watched James gently place Rose on a bench.

"You, Rose, Evan," Micah sighed. "Kevin and Riley texted that they're safe in the church next door."

"That's all of us?" Robby asked, desperate. He stood with his back against the glass wall. He could feel it vibrating. The chiming of the dawn bell could be heard just outside. The chaos and the pounding of the bloodlust-driven vampires merely escalated.

"Can you smell it?" James asked Micah. "You'll be down one more if you or I don't do this right now."

"Here?" Micah seemed revolted at the notion.

"What does he smell?" Robby asked, confused.

"Death. Vampires won't attack a dying person because there's no life-giving attributes to benefit them. In fact, it may weaken the vampire."

Robby dropped on his knees at the bench and held Rose's hand. "It's okay. They're going to fix it. No worries." Robby looked at James. "Micah has a plan to get us out of here. Can you do it?"

"I can. But I promise you, death would be better. For all of us," James warned. "I'm filled with self-loathing every night I have to go out and feed."

"I'll send her to a shrink," Robby joked in desperation.

James picked Rose up and placed her in Robby's arms. Gently brushing away her hair, James closed his eyes and bit Rose just behind the ear, then jerked away in revulsion. "That's awful. I've never tasted someone so close to death." He spit her blood onto the floor. James and Micah exchanged glances and nods.

Before Robby could comprehend what was happening, Evan was sinking to the floor with a tiny trickle of blood running down his neck. James smacked his lips. "That's better."

Micah stood over Robby. "Sorry, mate," he said through a very terrible forced accent, "but if I leave you in here alone with these two, you're a dead man."

Robby saw a blur of color, felt a pain in his chest, and then fell into darkness. He could hear everything in the blackness. Yet as soon as he heard it, he forgot it. There was the closing of the door as James and Micah left. He wondered where they would go. There was something coming, and another part of him, a new part, told him not to worry.

As Rose, Evan and Robby transitioned into immortality, another metamorphosis was happening above them in the stadium. There was the sound of cracking and pounding that soon transformed into the shattering of glass. A few humans made their way to the top windows of the old meat packing house, and clung to the metal grates, as their bodies were bathed in the sunlight of the rising sun. Others were not so fortunate.

Many humans, packed in, trapped and bleeding from shards of broken glass raining down on them, were a feast for the swarm of vampires that enveloped them. Women screamed as they were dragged down to the holding chamber and devoured in the relative darkness.

Some vampires took hostages and made them wait through the agonizing hours of the day until night fell again. When three consecutive nights had passed, every human who had watched *the game* was either drained of their blood, turned in the chaos, or was being kept for a future meal.

When Robby, Rose and Evan woke to their new selves three days later, they stepped out into the Detroit night. Ceremoniously, small groups of vampires were feasting on their human hostages. The smell of blood and fear was intoxicating. The three new vampires began to follow the scent in the hopes of a first feeding.

A screeching of tires erupted in the alley, and a Mercedes with pitch black windows came towards them, narrowly missing them and smoking its tires as it squealed to a stop. The back door opened and James grabbed Rose and Evan. When Robby leaned in to protest, he found himself stuffed in the back as well. The car took off as the door slammed shut.

James smiled wildly. "So sorry, I realize you three could use a proper meal. Half of the residents in this city will be slaughtered by morning. Because you're members of the undead now, it's not safe for you. We don't need you three added to the numbers when they find out who you are." He paused. "Or rather who you were. You may be one of us, but you did make vampires the laughing stock of our global society." Micah was driving fiercely as James tried to fill the three new vampires in after being gone for three days. He stopped to yell at Micah, "You're going the wrong way!"

"That group may have recognized them!" Micah argued.

"There's no time left for Kevin and Riley. Kevin texted an hour ago saying he wasn't sure if the parish priest had been killed or turned, but they'd heard commotion near their hiding place. Either way, their time has run out," James insisted.

"What are we going to do, put them in the Mercedes with three newly-turned vampires in the back seat?"

James thought for a minute. "Drop me off. Maybe I can protect them long enough for the three of them to feed. We'll have to hope their will is strong enough not to murder their friends when you come to pick us up."

Micah weaved in and out of back alleys, through streets and sidewalks filled with groups of young vampires traveling in small packs. As they rounded the corner near the church, Micah slammed on the brakes.

A woman had jumped from her apartment balcony and landed on the hood of the car from three stories up. She looked stunned and broken as she stared at Micah through the windshield.

Rose threw her head back as the smell of human blood hit her senses. Robby could feel his body begin to tremble at the rush of the bloodlust.

Evan pushed the handle of the door and was out before anyone could object. He pounced on the woman, unable to contain himself once the scent overtook him. She screamed, attracting little attention in what had become commonplace in the last seventy-two hours.

"So much for teaching them to feed discretely. Help Rose and Robby feed and get them back in the car. I'm going in for Riley and Kevin." James disappeared into the old, Detroit church while Micah tried to corral Robby and Rose.

As Evan drank from the thrashing woman on the car, he was rudely interrupted by a strong hand ripping him off her. He landed on the ground with a thud that was surprisingly not painful in the least.

"That was mine! I tracked her all the way to the balcony," a hideously ugly vampire said. He was clearly very old, with crustaceans or something similar to barnacles living on his face and hands. He hissed at Evan, barring his teeth angrily as he continued to rant. "I like mine half-broken. They don't fight so much when their backs are broken. Now learn to share young one, or I'll tell the new queen about you. She doesn't like those who take the lion's share for themselves."

Evan, slightly recovered mentally thanks to the life-restoring blood of his stolen prey, was quick to think. "Sorry, man, Detroit is a party. Food's everywhere! I thought food was falling from the sky, too!" He knew full well the more experienced vampire could probably kill him in a few short seconds.

The crusty vampire wiped a greasy wisp of long gray hair from his face and began to laugh. "Yes, I understand. I see your point, young one. Learn your manners or the authorities will force you to play a *game*." They both laughed; the old vampire in a friendly manner, Evan nervously.

As Evan slowly made his way back to the Mercedes, Micah had found an old couple hiding behind the church dumpster. Homeless and living off the charity of the churchgoers, they were well-concealed. Micah instructed Robby and Rose on the finer points of discretion and left them to their victims. The old couple shrank back in fear as Robby and Rose prepared for their first feeding.

Micah returned to the Mercedes and was relieved to find Evan already inside. Evan told of his encounter with the strange, ancient vampire.

Micah drummed his fingers on the steering wheel anxiously. If a queen had taken up some form of power, all the more reason to gather up Kevin and Riley and get the hell out of Detroit. Fires were beginning to glow as humans organized to retaliate. Two men stormed out of the apartment building across from the church with shotguns to reclaim the dead woman on the hood of the Mercedes.

Micah and Evan watched as they fired on the crusty vampire and his friends. The men fired repeatedly, taking turns shooting and reloading. The crusty vampire and his friends slowly walked towards the two rebellious men. The faster the men pumped lead into the slowly encroaching vampires, the larger the grins the vampires wore became.

"This town is becoming a war zone," Micah said. "What the fuck are Robby and Rose doing? All they had to do was kill the old couple and feed!" No sooner had he said it than Rose and Robby came into sight, emerging from the church alley.

They jumped into the back seat with Evan, Rose wiping her mouth with her sleeve. She checked Evan and Robby for blood on them as well, explaining she didn't want to scare Riley any more than they had to.

Micah texted James. It's safe. Get out here and hurry. This place is going to hell fast.

Inside the church, James struggled to catch the scent of human blood through the thick incense being burned at every corner of the building. He was surprised to find how very effective the smoky offering was in throwing him off. He texted Kevin but there was no response.

Analyzing the structure, he surmised that Kevin would likely have tried to hide Riley somewhere high, that he would tuck her into a tiny section near the attic and wait. James found the door to the choir loft and bounded up the stairs, calling out for Kevin and Riley openly. The chaos of the near riot outside was growing louder. James listened intently for any response inside the church. As he stood at the precipice of the loft, the door opened a little; a frail hand clung to the door knob.

A priest, standing with blazing eyes and blood-soaked robes, invited James in. He dropped to his knees and began to pray over a body that James regretfully recognized. It was Kevin.

"They thought it would be fun to see how long a priest could resist temptation," the vampire-priest whispered. "I thought I would hide myself away until the Heavenly Father found me fit to enter the gates of Heaven. But there they were. The two of them were hiding and I could smell their blood. I could hear their hearts thundering within their chests. It was as if Lucifer entered my body. My only salvation is that in my moment of doing the utmost evil, I chose the older man over the pure child," the priest confessed.

"Where's the girl?" James asked coldly.

"They took her."

"Who?" James shouted, his eyes blazing under his erupting temper. "Who took the girl?"

"She said she was the queen. The queen of vampires. She took the girl to be her subject for her Eternal Kingdom."

THE CONSERVATORY

By Michele Roger

After lying dormant for years, the Hillford Conservatory curse has risen from its blood-soaked foundations.

A student's corpse is found in the river with its arms cut off.

A nurse at the local hospital is found dismembered while the walls of the hospital bleed.

Students at the Conservatory have night terrors of being attacked by tiny blue creatures with scalpels and drills.

Some students say they see and hear the voice of a recently deceased student as the ghost haunts the school.

While the administration tries to save the reputation of the elite music conservatory, the gruesome secrets of Hillford begin creeping out.

But when a second student goes missing, it's up to Dr. Martin Lewis and music teacher Melody Steinwick to piece together the past in order to unravel the secrets of the present.

With death roaming the halls of Hillford, no one is safe.

THE PLACE TO GO FOR ZOMBIE AND APOCALYPTIC FICTION

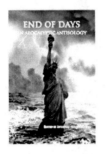

LIVING DEAD PRESS

WHERE THE DEAD WALK

www.livingdeadpress.com

CPSIA information can be obtained at www.ICGtesting.com
Printed in the USA
BVOW03s0719081014

369783BV00004B/10/P